I, Dr Greenblatt
Orthodontist,
251-1457

OTHER BOOKS BY GARY BARWIN

The Wild and Unfathomable Always (Xexoxial Editions, 2014)

Moon Baboon Canoe (Mansfield Press, 2014)

Franzlations: the Imaginary Kafka Parables. Collaboration with Hugh Thomas
   and Craig Conley (New Star, 2011)

O: eleven songs for chorus with Dennis Bathory-Kitsz (Westleaf Edition, 2011)

The Obvious Flap with Gregory Betts (BookThug, 2011)

The Porcupinity of the Stars (Coach House Press, 2010)

frogments from the frag pool: haiku after Basho with derek beaulieu (The Mercury
   Press, 2005)

Doctor Weep and Other Strange Teeth (The Mercury Press, 2004)

Raising Eyebrows (Coach House Books, 2001)

Outside the Hat (Coach House Books, 1998)

Big Red Baby (The Mercury Press, 1998)

Cruelty to Fabulous Animals (Moonstone Press, 1995)

The Mud Game, a novel with Stuart Ross (The Mercury Press, 1995)

FOR KIDS

Seeing Stars (Stoddart Kids, 2001)

Grandpa's Snowman (Annick Press, 2000)

The Magic Mustache (Annick Press, 1999)

The Racing Worm Brothers (Annick Press, 1998)

GARY
BARWIN

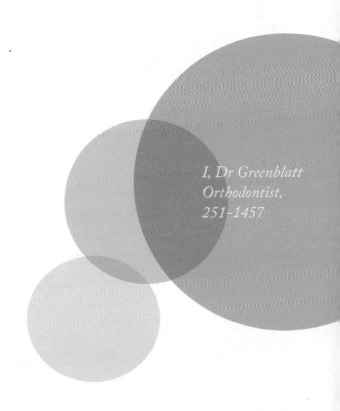

*I, Dr Greenblatt
Orthodontist,
251–1457*

ANVIL PRESS / VANCOUVER

Anvil Press Publishers Inc.
P.O. Box 3008, Main Post Office
Vancouver, B.C. V6B 3X5 CANADA
www.anvilpress.com

Library and Archives Canada Cataloguing in Publication

    Barwin, Gary, author
        I, Dr. Greenblatt, orthodontist, 251-1457 / Gary Barwin.

    Short stories.
    ISBN 978-1-77214-013-2 (pbk.)

        I. Title.

    PS8553.A783I12 2015   C813'.54   C2015-901620-7

Cover design by Rayola Graphic
Cover image by Gary Barwin
Author photo by Adele Talbot
Interior by HeimatHouse
Represented in Canada by the Publishers Group Canada
Distributed by Raincoast Books

The publisher gratefully acknowledges the financial assistance of the Canada Council for the Arts, the Canada Book Fund, and the Province of British Columbia through the B.C. Arts Council and the Book Publishing Tax Credit.

Who can open the doors of his face? his teeth are terrible round about.

— Job 41:13

The fourth generation of bees flee the unlocked mouth.

— Sherwin Bitsui

Hair and teeth. [You] got those two things [you] got it all.

— James Brown

1.

2.

3.

1.

THE RADIANT HAPPINESS

for my father

The doctor slept like a baby. Two women stood beside his bed. One tipped a bottle over a handkerchief and then covered the doctor's mouth and nose. The other pulled back the blankets and pushed a syringe through his navel. In this way, the baby began to grow inside the doctor. He did not understand the increasing bulge in his gut. In the beginning, he attributed it to a flourishing middle-age spread. Soon he felt the new heartbeat and then the kicking. It wasn't a kicking motivated by a need to escape, but rather an "I am here" call. Now I have intent and consciousness.

The baby was a constant companion for the doctor, a familiar kept safe and warm inside him. At times, the issue of orifices uncomfortably entered his mind. At some point in the future, his child would seek the world, a small cat looking for a cat-flap. Great pain or surgery would be required. In the meantime, the doctor took to wearing baggy clothing, oversized sweatshirts, and, while at work, white lab coats. Those around him noted the warm glow, the sense of bounty and health that radiated from his happy and larger self. When it seemed the doctor was speaking to himself, cheerily babbling about this or that—about birds or the moving clouds—his friends and office staff smiled indulgently, buoyed by his good humour and glad to overlook the quibbling eccentricity that so clearly originated in a deep pleasure and satisfaction with life itself.

The seasons passed. The baby grew. It took to ranging about the doctor's body, a restless toddler at play on a jungle gym. "Daddy, I love you," it said.

"Daddy, you are a good daddy. Daddy, I like it when you sing." And because he could not hold, or even see, his child, when the doctor was not explaining the vibrant surprises of the outer world, he sang almost non-stop: long improvised songs which incorporated the world and the doctor's feelings for his ever-growing child. The doctor's child was a bright, curious, and healthy child and continued to thrive. The doctor became massive, and though others shuddered when they observed his enormous misshapen body, he stumbled about with a fantastical grin transforming his unshaven chin. Five years passed. Fifteen. The child's voice changed. The doctor wrapped himself in vast cloaks and supported himself with canes and hid behind his desk during patient consultations.

Familiar as he was with the subtle distinctions of modern reproductive medicine, the doctor knew that this child could not be his own, or if it was, it had resulted from some surreptitious and unnatural sleight of—what might best be termed—hand. And the boy himself, who by now had developed a functional understanding of the basic operations of biological science, began to wonder in his liquid world about the nature of his own provenance. He was content within that fluid world—it was the only geography he had ever known—but the boy had begun to have longings concerning his own biology, about his own—though he hesitated to use the term with the doctor—mother.

The boy began to sing himself. Low-voiced songs of conjecture, filled with questions of metaphysics, of origin, and of the sports games of which he and his father were avid listeners. Might his mother, too, be a listener to these games? Might she participate in such games as a mother of his brother and sister? *Might* he have siblings? Did his brothers and sisters live on the outside, or did they too, live within another?

"Father, how was I conceived?" the boy asked the doctor one day between patients.

Though he knew much about the world and its reproductions, the doctor could not account or explain the boy's conception or, indeed, his arrival (biological or miraculous) inside of him. Superman's parents understood the spacecraft's implantation in the earth around Smallville. The doctor remembered only the small churnings, the ill feeling, the beginnings of movement. And the happiness. The radiant happiness.

THE HAND

I do not expect the hand. At first, I think it is a root or some other growing thing searching out food. I brush against it. It is cool though warmer than the air, warmer than the soil. I rest my head against its soft palm.

It cradles my head for hours, then it strokes my face. Perhaps it has a cramp and must move. I breathe, sleep, wake. The hand is gone. I sleep again.

When it returns, I touch my fingers to its fingers and they respond, curling. We remain fingertip to fingertip. I do not know for how long. My watch is gone. Nothing changes.

I sleep and when I wake, the hand has disappeared. My fingers are empty. I feel for the hole in the earth where the hand has returned. There are several small crevices and I reach in. Nothing but dirt or vacancy. Somewhere in this country, they think of shoes, stationery, a plate of meat, the floor of a change room.

Then I feel the hand against my side. I hold it. We are parent and child, sisters, lovers walking together, watching the moon, anticipating the boat which will take us across the river. We whisper our stories. We are silent.

The hand is the moon, clouds. A sigh. I begin to wait for it. To expect. It is a television. A friend. What does it hope for, reaching, holding, sharing its quiet?

Fields of daisies, butterflies, explosives. There is no remembering. A cubicle. The Canadian Shield, its stunted trees and shine of mica. Burritos, librarians, snakes, and nightstands. Documents passed from hand to hand in secret.

The hand carries nothing. Heat. A body. Happiness. I feel little except when I hold the hand. It could not have been looking for me, could not have anticipated finding me. A human hand among thousands: its own shadow, cold, sightless, underground; its mother, master, child, slave. Its twin.

I outline letters on its palm, but it does not understand. Its fingers move. Maybe it writes, but were it Arabic or English, I feel only caresses and swirls. An intimate and inscrutable grammar.

We lock our fingers together. We sleep. Wake. Are happy.

After a few days, the hand does not appear, I think I have lost my own hand. Later, I realize, the hand is gone. Hand. Gust of wind. The wide earth. Death. Someone brings me food.

I open and close my own hand. I open and close it. I pass the memory of the hand between each of my own hands. What can be held in a hand, what has flown away? I remember nothing.

MAHONEY LONESOME

The victorious wrestler is an oiled rhinoceros in a green Speedo, stomping the ground with his delicate feet. His funeral barge arms are ceremoniously poised above the golden sheaves of his mullet, shorn and curled like an offering in a rite of vegetative fertility. His muscles are burial mounds beneath the roiling prairie of his taut and blushing skin. His is the roar of a locomotive in pain, an avalanche of rocks crushing the family car.

His broad box-spring torso is a queen bed of slats, sleek and lumpy as after the coitus of mammoths. And the crowd, furious with enthusiasm, creating a broadband hiss like the white noise rush of the universe collapsing at the end of time, has filled the air with the reckless sacrifice of their larynxes and tongues, an exuberant abattoir of joy and rage.

But let's talk about viruses. The tiny Whoville network of viruses on the wrestler's tight trunks. Or one single virus, living at the end of a cellular cul-de-sac, attempting to seek life and to flourish, to find meaning and satisfaction, here on the brief green earth. The virus is a single word in the great wiki of hope and information, a mortal sleeperhold in spacetime, an earnest Tonga deathgrip on life. In the big world, there may be the end-of-days tectonic supernovae of bodyslams, the torque of tiger feint crucifix armbars on the topology of subspace, but the virus perseveres in its ardent intracellular replications, its ontological infections, its almost-endless epistemology of transmission.

They call our virus, Mahoney Lonesome, and it works its covert operations in the crawlspace beneath the organic stairs, a childlike and surreptitious spectator between parents in the interstellar parade of microscopic communication. It is both mail carrier and letter, firefighter and fire, gravity and galaxy.

It is a long and a short story. The Klieg lights of the ring have been silenced, night achieved by a switch, and the wrestler returns home. Another human, child or lover, rushes to greet him. The Red Sea parts in an exodus of blood and memory, and the virus takes its plagues wandering into the desert of the other. Mahoney Lonesome, a shadow, a spirit, the jubilation of souls in contact, enters the other, a certain knowledge, a chinlock, the sun shining into night, a cobra clutch, a front chancery of love, forgetfulness, immunity, or chance. There is a vacant region in spacetime, bounded by ropes or string theory, which remains vacant but which will always remember. If the crowd believed it could exist in twenty-two dimensions, there'd be cheering.

COFFEE, NEWSPAPER, EGGS

There were two of us, but we had only one pair of legs. We took turns walking. I'd walk into the park that was crammed with leaves and butterflies and good smells. Then I'd walk home and tell you all about it. Later, you'd walk to the mall. It was stuffed full of skirts, cellphones, Chinese food, and hooded sweatshirts. You'd march right up the stairs where I would be in the big chair, waiting to hear all about your adventure. I'd put down my newspaper and you'd tell me everything. Ginger chicken—really?

Some might wonder why we couldn't just share one leg each. We tried. We learned to hop. We wrapped our arms around each other's shoulders and pretended to be a big double person with a single set of legs, but it wasn't the same. We didn't feel right separating the legs. They belonged together. Like Laurel and Hardy, Brad Pitt and Julia Roberts, spic and span, left and right, Google and Yahoo, and the two of us.

In the summer, our house was surrounded by millions of yellow flowers. It was because of us. People drove by our house, real slow, just to look at our flowers. In spring you'd take the legs out into the garden and dig a bunch of holes. Then you'd walk in and have a glass of lemonade at the kitchen table and wipe your sweaty brow. Ahh, you'd say. Your turn, you'd say, and I'd take the legs and carry out armfuls of flower bulbs. I'd stick the bulbs into the millions of holes that you'd dug. Look. You forgot the shovel beside the apple tree. It's OK. I'll carry it to the garage. I have the legs.

We bought shoes online so that we could both be involved in the selection of footwear. I preferred the convenience of Velcro but you, if you had your druthers, would opt for classic lace-ups. It was black for me. White for you. Invariably we settled on slip-ons in light brown. I don't want you to think that it wasn't a rich life, a vivid and satisfying life, a life of rich imagination and personal choice. Ours was a vibrant tango of intersecting free will, a mambo up the relationship decision tree.

One day, the sun shone into our window like a searchlight. It woke us both up. Hey, I said. I'll take the legs and go downstairs and make some coffee, then you can go and get the paper. Then I'll make the eggs. OK, you said. But first let me go to the bathroom. OK, I said. That necessarily has to come before coffee. Yes, you said. Without question. So I'll wait, I said. Yes, you said. What else would you do? Handsprings, I said.

We looked around but the legs were gone. Maybe they wriggled under the bed? I asked. They were not under the bed. Maybe you left them in the walk-in closet? you asked. But they were not in the walk-in closet. Could we have left them in the nursery? we wondered. Once, many years ago, we had hoped to have a baby together. We would have shared our baby like our legs. You would go to the Christmas Concert and see our baby sing. I would go to meet-the-teacher night and hear about our little one's progress with scissors. While you tucked her into bed, I would sing from the other room. But the legs were not in the nursery. Not in the garden. Not in the mall. I used the telescope and looked all over. You used your wide-ranging psychic powers to determine that the legs were not in the park.

This marks a significant change in our lives, I said. Without legs, we are different, you said. We lay in our bed and clung together. The sun rose far into the sky like a soccer ball kicked too high over a goalpost. Then it fell down to the pink horizon and we were in darkness. The next day, it did it again. We did not leave the bed. Your arms were wrapped around my torso. My arms were wrapped around your torso. Each of our shoulders, both our left and our right, were wet with each others' tears. A month passed. Then ten years. We suspected the loss of millions of flowers but neither of us had the mental stamina nor the psychological agility to look.

Why had our legs left us? Where had they gone? We imagined them at a restaurant table in Los Angeles wearing aviator sunglasses and ordering an expensive imported water with lemon. Maybe they were in India, helping the poor. A pair of legs could make a difference there, we reasoned. A significant difference. But it had been so sudden. They had left without warning. There was no note, no phonecall, not even a footprint left on the front walkway. By now, the legs must have changed. We'd probably not recognize them if they walked right up to us and knelt down. The world was large and a pair of legs could choose to live anywhere, could choose to live almost any story. It was not fair of us to want to hold the legs back, to not allow the legs to realize their own personal and innate legness. To be with other legs. To feel the hot wind of Iceland blowing against their knees, the unrelenting prickle of the Antarctica's sand against their pale calves, to feel the muscular pleasures of making a jump shot at the end of an inning late in the evening at a Tokyo ballpark, the fans standing and waving their colourful scarves. Somewhere in this large blue world, the legs were happy. It was time we understood that.

How? you asked. How are we going to do without the legs?

We'll find a way, I said. First coffee. Then eggs.

THE GREAT EXPLORER

The great explorer leaves the palace. Even without his splendid hat of feathers, he has to crouch to get through the gates.

"Those at the gates are the brothers of explorers," he says to the gatekeeper. "We look into the distance and see first what others see only later."

"Sometimes I see those who return with an arrow stuck through them," the gatekeeper says. "Though mostly I sleep in this chair with my hat pulled over my eyes."

The explorer mounts his horse and rides out into the fields. He smells the scent of rolled hay, sees the familiar pocketful of stars.

Then he rides to the shore and boards his ship. He will find a new land. Those on the shore watch him sail away. They watch him get smaller as he approaches the horizon. He is the size of a small child. Soon he is no bigger than a pebble. Then he is nothing but a speck, a pinprick, a molecule.

He sails across the sea and discovers a new land. He throws down his anchor then rows to shore. An island chief appears on the sand. He is surrounded by many people dancing and bearing great platters of fruit.

The island chief looks around the shore. He looks at the sea. He looks up, then down. Then he sees the explorer.

"These platters of fruit are for you, small one," the chief says.

"Thanks," the explorer says. "They look delicious."

"Might take a few days to eat them," the chief says. "What with your size and all."

"What about my size?" the explorer asks.

"My brother, you are very small," the chief says. "Like a mosquito or an electron. But do not worry. My own son was born small. At first we thought he was just far away. But eventually he grew. Though he's still ugly, even from a distance. Monkey-face, we call him."

"Your people dance well," the great explorer says.

"You are so small, but have come so far," the chief replies.

"I can't afford to get smaller. I might disappear. Have my ship," the explorer tells the chief. "The next world is yours."

THE SLEEP OF ELEPHANTS

for Melanie Drane

On its side, half-covered in blanket, the elephant fills the bed, its slow breathing the surrender of lungs, a confession. The elephant is a form of twilight, its shadow skin, cobweb-coloured. I am a road, grey and endless, leaving the fog-bound house. I am an elephant also, if only in solidarity.

World, I say, your parking meters and slate roofs, your storm clouds and uncertainties, pencil leads and rain. You have always been elephantine, winding through the half-lit maze, your baleful trumpeting and subaudible song. Mouse, you whale of the wainscot, bat, you whale of dusk, you are elephants seen through the multifaceted eyes of insects. All roads are elephants, all bathtubs, laundromats, and reference texts. What is plural is elephant. What is singular. A rural road, I fly alone in the night sky, itself a dark road with no border but the horizon and the rich elephantine earth, a constellation of shadows.

I find a pillow, half-buried beneath the vast foreleg of the elephant. I lie down beside the elephant which is dying. I do not hear, but feel the elephant's murmuring, the worlds it speaks in consolation, time, a kind of twilight articulated in sound. I sleep beside its universe, its inhalations and outbreaths, a slow expansion and contraction of the rolling curves of its body. If there are stars, they have closed their eyes, they are past shining outward.

Elephant, old man, old woman, what is beyond old man and woman. Landscape, helium, dust; settlement, spacetime, nest. Let us be governed by twilight, or the twilight of twilight which is a shadow in the mirror. Elephant, there are others, too, who will find you, who will bring you the consolation of sleep. The somnolent rest with you, march beside you into night. And when you turn, deep in your dream, our crushed bones will become, like a comet's dust, a radiant trail of loss and return, an elephant.

POLAR BEAR

A man flew across an ocean. He flapped hard. There would be new things across the sea. In fact, there would be amazing newness. Polar bears, new people, electronic marvels. There would be his mother. After one week, the man landed in our country. He had a tin can and a string which once connected it to another tin can, but with all the flapping, the string had broken. Now he was in our airport with an empty can and his words were strange. The airport didn't like his can and his broken string.

"Don't carry too much liquid," the airport said. "Remember your tray table," the airport said. "Don't use strange words," the airport said. "And take off your shoes."

The man wanted to get out of the airport but the airport wouldn't let him. "Please," the man said, but the airport said, "No."

"Please?" the man said.

"No," the airport said. "Not yet."

"How about now?" the man said.

But the airport said, "Not yet," and made him wait some more.

The man wanted to get out of the airport. It did not like him. He waited six months. Then he held up a stapler and a small table. He was waiting for his mother, for polar bears, for electronics. Surely a country as beautiful could not keep him from polar bears, electronics, and his mother, he thought.

We police were big but we were not yet polar bears. "We are going to shout things," we said. "And you will understand." We began shouting but the man did not understand. "Now we will shout again," we said. "We will shout louder and we will order you to understand. And just to be safe," we said, "we will lock your hands together. Don't thank us. Don't applaud. It is our job." The man did not thank us or applaud. One should only clap when things are over, he thought.

We were not his friends. The airport didn't like him. Then we plugged him into the ground. An electronic marvel. A fistful of storm turning his bones to flesh, his flesh to bone. He fell to the floor. A man made squid. Then he died. An amazing newness. An ocean. A tin can big as the world.

This is what happened. This is my evidence. I am a polar bear, a police officer, some broken string. I did not applaud.

FLIGHT PATH

In my country, two men often marry. Two women also. And these people are happy or not, in the manner of any marriage or of any couple throughout the world or time.

And so the time came for me, when I, too, was seized with the desire to marry. But I wanted something closer than holly and ivy, closer than two sprigs of holly, or two vines of ivy. Something closer than bread and toast. Something more like breathing.

So I married myself.

Marriage is like a Möbius strip, a twisting, turning thing that appears to have two sides, but, in reality, has only one. Or that appears to have only a single side, but in truth has two. It's the edges that are important. It's the edges that are often forgotten.

It was a beautiful day. There was music. In the man-made glade, there was a flute and a harp. Or two harps. Or a single flute. There was a rabbi. A single rabbi with a snow-cloud beard like Santa Claus. There were piles of food and an ice sculpture in the shape of God and Adam pointing at each other from the ceiling of the Sistine Chapel. In the middle of the boundless sweet table, there was a three-tiered wedding cake, and at its summit, under a little icing-sugar chuppah, a single person in a black tuxedo. This, in the language of celebration and the alchemy of cake-decoration, was me. After the traditional ceremony on the stage of the lovely country chapel, I embraced myself and cried as I promised to be true to this life before God, my parents, my friends, and myself. Then I stomped on the wine glass and the people broke into song.

My love was not absolute, for life is changeable, uncertain, a minefield of betrayals and tragedy. But I had faith. I had the courage of my promise. I would forever be true to this love, whether it flickered or shone bright. Whether it was a candle or a Klieg light. Whether it was a Klimt or a Sigmund Freud. My love for myself would deepen with time. There would be therapy, counselling, and walks by the sea as the sun set. I thought how the sand was like the ripples I felt as I touched my tongue to the roof of my mouth and explored.

I gave myself pleasure, laughed at my own jokes. Sometimes, I knew what I was thinking; sometimes, I did not. After a while, it became more difficult to surprise myself, but I managed. I was a man of routine, but then, without warning, I would change. I'd find myself across town eating somewhere new, trying something different. Is this sea cucumber? I've never had sea cucumber. I'd take in the ballet or a ball game. Sometimes within an hour of one another. I would add spice to things that never had spice. I would dress in the dark, only open my eyes downstairs before the mirror. I would write notes to myself without looking. I learned to speak without first thinking, learned to anticipate my every need. I appreciated the little things. Is that a new tie? I can't believe what you managed on that triple-word score.

I filled my house with mirrors so I was surrounded by love. In some places where there were two mirrors, it seemed that there were an infinite number of marriages, my life a Ziegfeld Folly down a connubial corridor, a blissful kaleidoscope of spouses waving at each other, looking out with endless pairs of eyes into the same happy and domestic world.

There were years of happiness. Holidays. Promotions. Birthdays. Good times, with friends and alone. A new house. A cottage by the sea. Late night drives out into the country, nothing but the stars, the empty fields, and thoughts intertwined with the quiet songs of the radio. Sunday morning coffee on the porch or in bed. Dreams shared. The prosody of reality scanned. New family. Crises met, averted, or suffered.

I was taken by surprise when the news came, though I had not been feeling well and had been taking it easy, pacing myself, spending more time at home, and at rest. But still, I was young. I felt strong, and there was much to do, much to look forward to. Soon it would be spring. There was gardening. The crocuses had bloomed between the mess of dried stalks in last year's gardens. A niece and a nephew were learning to roll over, to walk, beginning to name things, to delight in their new discoveries. My parents had become warm and sentimental, feeling joy and satisfaction in their family and each other, now having time to deeply experience each small trouble or accomplishment. And my marriage. I looked forward to an old-age marriage: of cups of tea carefully carried to the bedside, of memories dim yet strongly felt, of fastidious preparation on the calendar for each minor outing or appointment.

The doctor said there was not much time. Maybe a month. Maybe only two weeks. I thought back to the day of my wedding. I don't know why but I remembered the stains on the waiters' white jackets, the cloying questions of the videographer, my brother's bad jokes, the beautiful lithe body of an old friend from college, and my own young self. There was the future like the inconceivably long flight path of a migrating bird. A path stretched out before endless generations of birds. Each bird could not conceive of the distance of its destination or of the vastness of its route, but knew only the winds, the position of the stars, and some kind of deep pull from far inside its brain.

At the end, I sat myself up in the wheelchair and waited. The nurse helped me dress and shave. I brushed my hair carefully and put on cologne. I was as handsome as I'd ever been.

BICYCLE

Somewhere in the world is the bicycle which I abandoned for a reason it did not understand then, and, leaning in the half-dark shed at the end of the garden, covered in cobwebs, it still cannot quite fathom. Its plaintive handlebars, slightly stooped, shrug resignedly, turned toward the bent-nail wall. Small wrinkles show the years of sadness felt by the forehead-sized seat, now twisted somewhat off-centre as it remembers the cheeks of my little apple-round boy bottom, the touch of my pale white hands. One day, we were chased by Lindsay Neville after escaping from his tree house; another, distracted by a shout, we rode full force into a hedge-covered wall. Together we rode into the wind and out of the neighbourhood after my grandfather's funeral. Many times, we combed the twisting paths of the subdivision noting each tonal shift of street and crescent, of painted garage door and window trim, of cedar hedge, rock garden, and lamppost. One day, I leaned the bicycle against the side of the house and walked away. One day I'd become taller, older, and my father had promised me another.

NEW FACE

Pain is almost everywhere. Across my forehead, my lips, my head and neck. It radiates from my bones. The broken ends of my arms. But there is less of it. There's a bench in the park where I have made it my custom to sit each day. I watch the people walking by. The mothers with strollers and the skitter of toddlers running ahead of them. The seniors walking alone or together.

They gave me a new face. They tried to give me new hands but they did not take and they had to be removed. With my new face, I smiled, sadly. Thanks for trying, I said without irony.

My old face was taken by a chimpanzee. My best friend's pet. Not any less painful because absurd and bizarre.

I go outside with my new face and smile. I walk in the park, under the dappled light between trees. I'm frightening to children. Disconcerting to adults. But I have a face. I am alive. I can smile. It's both a more complicated and a simpler smile than before, but I am able.

The chimp destroyed my hands, also.

Hello, Mrs. Bachman. Good morning Mr. Sam. How ya doing, Jimmy?

Times I would take that chimp in my old hands and squeeze its hairy throat until with the chimp gurgling for air, I hear the bones of its neck crack and the chimp a limp potato sack falls to the ground. Times I'd take its pink wrinkled face in my old hands and bite until it bleeds and is pulled off and is an unrecognizable Silly Putty pulp, a face scalped and flattened like roadkill driven over again and again by traffic. No, wait. It was between me and the chimp. But not in that order.

It has been years of doctors, surgeries, and pain killers. I have been a battle field. The doctors, my family and I trusting knives, lasers, blood and ourselves. When the soldiers and their machines go home, I am a broken place where someone has put up a sign saying remember what happened here. But I never left. I remember.

THE ASCENSION OF MS. PAC-MAN

for A.G. Pasquella

The wind and sea beyond my hospital room window. Ah the birds, the children, the husks of ex-lovers rolling over tarmac, the weeping of chauffeurs, the luminous exoskeletons of ghosts and octopi. The moon is my haunted body, yellow and round against the dark warp of night's black tunnel.

Once I was ripe. Once I patrolled the mazes. Once the energizers were inside me and the ghosts were vulnerable. O 100 point pair of cherries. O pears, pretzels, O bonus fruit.

I look toward my dinner tray and weep. O Chaser, Ambusher, Fickle, O Stupid. O Urchin, Romp, Stylist, O Crybaby. I am a crone, a hag, a gorgon. I was a shark, eating light in order that I could live. O Shadow, Speedy, Bashful, Pokey. O Blinky, Pinky, Inky, O Clyde, my lovers. O you 5000 point banana. Life is a subroutine that draws only erroneous fruit and never solace or a peaceful, victorious, numberless end.

All my youth, I floated through a labyrinth of dupes and chumps. I sought the skeletons of life's ghosts, the lightning-blue monsters of sex, consumption, and the tailless pellets of Pac-Man's jizz, its unending ellipses indicating absence only. And now, I am a pale and fulvous Tiresias of the sheets being fed only peas in the narrow maze of silver guardrails around this single bed. Immobile. Forgotten. My once red lips pallid and deflated, my buttery legs sallow pixels only.

O witch world of three dimensions. O ray of light. O quick fingers. I feel your breath upon me. I know my soul which turned as a red bow upon my vacant brow will soon unravel and journey toward the heavens where I shall speak my own name and travel the edgeless rounds of star fields, alone in the emulation of infinite space.

THE HAIRCUT

Each hair is equal, each hair is entitled to the same rights, privileges and caresses by fingers and the wind as every other hair, his father had said. And so, he would honour his father. His hair would not be the uneven and unfair coiffure of the past. It would be new hair: long, equal, and proud.

The other kids did not understand. They carried him to the woods in a cardboard box and buried him beside an old sofa.

On Monday, in darkness, he imagined the innumerable grasses of his scalp's savannah. On Tuesday, a vast prehistoric fern rising from the verdant forest floor of his organically vibrant head. Wednesday: prize wheat on the tractless blond prairie of his pink pate. By Thursday, he knew that this was another impossible dream. One of his hairs was different. It grew faster than the others. It was magnificent.

Sunday night, it broke the earth's surface and he emerged from his paper tomb.

He went straight home and stayed there. He could not leave, for though he had had an extensive style and trim, a short back and sides, a buzz, a perm, a treatment, the one hair again became huge and snaked through the rooms of his house like the black power cords of the many morning talk show film crews who visited him, freakishly imprisoned within his small and now rather unkempt bedroom. For as it had grown, the fame of this single marvellous hair had grown also. The crowds surrounded his house, congregated in his yard, disturbed the neighbours, searching for hairnets, for product, for discarded, and possibly unrecognized, remarkable hairs. The people came from throughout the land, from over the seas, from salons with blue comb-desterilizer water and scented brushes.

His hair grew until it was an antenna extending around the world, the world in its normal-to-oily embrace. Children played beside the hair. They held sections and played jump rope. One-a-daisy. Two-a-daisy. Let's step in.

But the hair divided villages. It was a wall through the main street. Animals, coming across the hair in the midst of migration mistook it for an oil pipeline, changed their route and died. His father would not be proud, though his hair had become a symbol of the earth's pugnacious fertility, it had also become a security fence between nations. The Nobel Prize committee awarded his hair the Peace Prize only so they could disgrace the hair by taking it back. Generals met in secret to discuss plans to develop electrolysis from space. But still the hair grew.

The children who had buried him talked to each other from the computers in their rooms. They schemed. Something had to be done.

His hair now reached beyond the earth and was as a comb-over for Jupiter. What would happen, they demanded, if the hair curled and began to crowd out the sun?

We need the hair, he told them. The hair is everything: good and evil, memory and prediction. It is the spirit of animals, lined up, one after the other as if waiting for a movie, the drainpipe of space spiked bright with stars. It is a hundred Deaths descending the Playland slide, dark robes fluttering, their shoeless feet pulled up close, the howling throat of a toddler-minded man remembering spring. We need the long hair, he said. It is the ever-growing black stem of a daisy sent from the future to remind us who we are and who we might be. We are equal, he said, but only with ourselves and our futures. The hair is a long finger and it is pointing at us.

The children went into their backyards and looked toward heaven. Satellites moved across the sky, dodging the giant hair. Wind from over the fence tousled the children's bangs.

We believe you, they said. We love you.

2.

STREAMBED

for Aaron Barwin

A cloudless day in the cemetery where we have gone for a funeral. Our five-year-old, named after his late grandfather, wanders about the headstones, dragging his fingers along the streambeds of carved-out letters. He stumbles upon his own name inscribed above a small bed of grass. He lies down, crosses his arms, closes his eyes, and waits. In time, he becomes old. The wind carves his features smooth as river rock. Someone lifts him and places him on his grandfather's headstone. We no longer remember the town where he was born.

NEWS

There is a man covered in glass on the lawn of a burning house. Soon there are sirens and then ambulances, police, firefighters. Inside the house, three children, a wife, a dog, covered in stab wounds.

They take the family into the forest and turn them into trees. They have dark branches with deep green leaves. The man becomes a river, its cool water flowing over the twisted brown roots of the family.

There's a bird, a bird with messy black feathers. It flies into town and into the office of the newspaper reporter. Make all stories like this one, it says.

CHINA

In bed, China is a baby kitten. India purrs expectantly. America twists on its back, shows me its belly. They're jealous. Here China. Here's milk. Let me scratch you. Let me love you, poor frail thing. Come under my long moustache, China, for it protects those over which its thin shadow falls. My rock 'n' roll hydroelectric brain, my bird's nest calligraphic heart. Each border between cell wall and cell wall, the delicate tracing of ink. A nostalgia for a future. China, there you were on my doorstep. Your thin cry, your scrabbling paws. The moon is a superpower. I hold you in my arms, whisper to your economy, your ecological disaster, your hope. China, the world is a superpower. We comfort each other.

BODY BAG

There was cake and candles. Singing and then some gifts.

"Here," his parents said. "Your body bag."

When it was over, he walked into the schoolyard. There were birds in the trees. Dogs ran across the soccer field. The bag was rolled like a sleeping bag and tucked under his arm. It was rough canvas, taller than him, and with a brass zipper. He carried it with him. On the bus. Bike riding. Hiking. While sleeping. He left it outside the stall during showers and on the deck while he swam. Beside his desk during school. Under his chair during meals.

Soon he was forty. The same sky. Different birds. Other dogs. Sometimes he unrolled it and laid it out on his floor. Pale, expressionless, empty. He never looked inside to see where he would go. He was now the same size as the bag. Pale, also, but paunchy, thick and prone to exhaustion. Once he climbed a mountain and the bag went with him. Once he had surgery and it lay beside the operating table in a sterilized bag of its own.

Then he was ninety. He wandered through the schoolyard where many trees had fallen. Many birds and dogs. He remembered his parents with tenderness. It was time for the body bag. He unrolled then unzipped it a little. He gathered soil and pushed it into the bag. He wrote his name on a stone and put it inside also. He cut himself the length of his belly, buried the bag inside, then stitched himself up.

He lay down on the grass and died.

ICEMAKERS OF THE ANTEATER

An anteater chews through the house. The chair arms. Glasses. The legs of chairs. The mattress. It's the boyfriend my nine-year-old daughter's going to have ten years from now. It chews up the swimming pool. I sit on the porch throwing toasters, and shout, "Don't ever come back!" From under its coat, the boyfriend takes out a violin and begins to play some obscure anteater song. Then my daughter appears from the roots of a burning tree, dressed in football equipment. The sun, in an obvious attempt at drama, backlights her with its crimson tongue. She crouches low and then rushes against the house. It falls, a sack of doleful rooms, stairs and carpeting. The anteater splits in half. From its insides are born three angels, white as fridges, icetrays hidden between their cloud-like wings. In each tray are my daughter's future children, tiny, curled up, and frozen.

THE SKY ABOVE CHAIRS

The chair nuzzles against trees. It remains still, invisible to its predators. Looking is a contract between hunter and hunted. Also, hiding. Look at a chair. It looks back, waiting for what's next. The desk chair. The chair of another. The chair at rest.

A forest of chairs, a silent choir, the inverse of trees yet becoming trees. Moist pools of thought or sense. Inside the chair, a red city, a briefcase, an underground of blood.

Once, a house where chairs were everything. In bed. The garage, the rec room. Small childhood chairs. In the attic. In the breakfast nook. Old man chair. New baby chair. The carpets were chairs. Remember when we were young? When did they come to our home, the forest the size of humans, not chairs?

Once, in early spring, the chairs were in our yard. We spoke in whispers, as if before a house of cards. The chairs seemed telepathic, each thought shared between the group of chairs. They waited as one, then leapt the fence in a single thought, a flock of birds, their wings silent and invisible.

In the ravine, leaves unfurl, branches complete their plans. Clouds hunt the moon as the moon hides then disappears. We know the chairs are moving, but see only dust motes illuminated in a beaming slash of forest light, the scuttle of leaves on the forest floor, a scurry like the word 'chair' whispered from nearby. Chairs, we say. Goodbye.

THE LOLLYGAGGING PRONGS OF THE SIX-BAR BLUES

It is a rainy Saturday afternoon and we're sprawled on a couch, sipping coffee. Love is a bright fork retrieving pickles, Fred says, munching on a sandwich. Or else it is a radiant pickle waiting to be touched by lollygagging prongs ferreted from the miniature display case at the nocturnal end of sorrow's long hallway.

And I say: it is a set of hopeful teeth swooping into the open mouth of a howling candy-store wolf, causing its loping face to whistle into the pickle-sweet air. It is an air-conditioner strapped to the back of a convenience store clerk clipping roses in the red velvet bag of yesterday's arboretum.

But George says: No. It is a sticker of Snow White stuck to the left arm of a solar-powered electric chair lost in a mine-shaft below the deli. It is a librarian sawing a harmonica in half with a bread knife. And, he says, love hurts.

If you're the harmonica, Fred says.

The couch is in the middle of an intersection. We are three friends and let's just say that each of us are playing two sets of the six bar blues, expecting Barbie, or Bambi, or Baden-Powell to arrive with flags instead of sorrow on the city bus bound for the lake of sudden frogs.

BULLET

On the day of my birth, my father pushes his gun through the upstairs window and shoots a goose from the sky.

Now they gather like specialists around my bed. Dr. Cumulus with his hailstone forceps, Northern Lights with her shimmering tray of Poptarts and moonshine, Moon picking his teeth with the TV guide, rubbing his chin on the back of morning.

They say that soon the goose will crash through the ceiling and we will meet for the first time, the goose only bones or the dust of bones, and I too, not more much more than dust.

I wonder: Who will pay for the hole in the roof? With what will they shingle? And my father's bullet, once it has pierced then travelled beyond the goose, where will it go?

On the next mountain over, my cousin Hans carries a bucket of milk from the goat of grandma, resting by the fire. A sound like a bell in the church then his left toe explodes in a fireworks of pain, then blood, and a stream of goat milk engulfs his foot, flowing pink and warm down into the dusty valley.

BRAVE CAPE

Everything is dark, as if life depended upon a lump of coal in the sky instead of a sun. Sight is a black fog. I am huge and cold. I can't breathe. My mouth is stone. My nose rigid: a carrot, a turnip, a stone. My arms, never athletic, are twigs. My feet have disappeared. I am perhaps the only snowman. In the sharp air, only blue shadows. I know that in a blind world, there is infinite regression, each blind dog relying on another blind dog to lead it forward through the velvet-shadowed gardens. A dog lifts its leg to me. I can't close my eyes.

Instead, I switch them, the left and the right. I replace my eyes with the stones of my mouth. I replace the vast ball of my legs with my torso ball. My sad head rolls down the hill and becomes enormous and quick as it descends. Such a large head can imagine great things. Melting, for instance. Small children squashing living things. The possibility that their family, slowly, unsteadily, shall cross the frozen sea, that Miranda shall fight the wind with her cape and thus save Timmy from the treacherous ground, the squat fingerprints of his future.

I crash into a fence. I lose track of my head. I become blue light. Then rain.

MY NOBEL PRIZE

They stick the real Nobel Prize to my chest. The pin goes through my heart. Don't worry: it's made of a material that I just invented. It is both wife and participle. Royal jelly and particle board. It is shadow and light rolled into one like chocolate, riot gear or the end of the world.

In fact, I recently invented myself. I am entirely new. A new cloud, a new ant. Hook me up to the flat screen IV and let the 3D beam through my veins like weather. Change my channel. I sleep.

I said, the mind is a lawnmower chewing up lawn. There was a dog in that yard. It was a problem but it is a problem no more. That's why my heart got pinned with this prize. My mind-blades ran over something no one else noticed, but I don't throw away the bags. I am all new.

Newsflash: Nobel Prize pin insertion causes end of world. The end is very small. It's far away. You would need a giant's telescope or death-defying binoculars to see it. They thought we would all die. There are clouds over my tongue.

An enormous whale or a bean from the edge of the universe, a universe that still doesn't have a name because it keeps getting bigger. I invented bigger. And I forgot my newness because I invented it so fast I finished before I began. I said to the universe, You can't kill me because only one of us is going to die due to some kind of spacetime thing which is very complicated and that only I can explain.

Yes, you should thank me for receiving this prize with my only heart. My words are shadows in my hands. Now I open them and let the dove that was never there become something small and far away, far away as the end of the world. In conclusion, Mr. and Mrs. Committee, I'd like to begin by inventing someone else. All this new gets lonely.

NO STORY NEITHER

O tiny flower-sized washing-machine alphorn Hans set up high in the hills because the Miniature Village laundromat closed down, and Greta left for Munich with a travel agent.

O delicate bee-bedecked Maytag spinning in the golden alpine light, a mystery to villagers who far below appear as nine point type milling about the snowy foolscap of the village, you signal to the ghosts it is time to come home.

Yes, the virtuoso twist of your rinse cycle—a liquid country-song cyclone—calls and the ghosts remember the moment of birth, the comfort of straw, their dirty clothes strewn around the meadow and think of Greta, the way her blue eyes crackled when, from his chosen landromat machine, Hans produced with a flourish, a perfectly clean yet singing flower. Come home. Come home. Come home.

RAT

There is a large rat in our house. It gnaws at our feet. It crawls under the sheets of our beds as we sleep. It sits at the table while we eat. It doesn't say, "Pass the bread," but climbs up the tablecloth and chews at the food, its tail curling into the salad.

"Is it grandpa?" my daughter asks.

"No," we say. "It is a rat."

"Let's give it a name."

"No," we say. "It is a rat."

"Then we must kill it," our youngest says. "I will drown it in the bath."

Instead, my wife and I dig a hole in the middle of the living room. We gather blankets and pillows. The family climbs in and we cover ourselves up. "Who will remember us?" we ask.

3.

THE DISHWASHER AND THE BILLIONAIRE

for Jacob Wren

We lie in bed together. I'm almost a cube, my tubes still connected. My racks: beautiful, capacious, light blue. Nothing in the soap compartment, control panel buttons illuminated green, my spinner like helicopter blades made of beluga. He sleeps.

The morning sun shines. Below us, the distant chimes like sink-washed wine glasses. We're under blankets. What is our life? Open sky. Love like sheets drying slowly, scented by wind, billowing or swaying, the outside moving through.

A smile on his lips, patchy hair on his chest. The boy he was, discovering himself. I am made of small Phillips screws, cruciform, plastic, and stainless steel. I remember the middle ages. What is this money? There was a horse. A joke. I crossed a river.

How do we speak? The ocean waves sleep, my billionaire, the banks of infinite stars nearly within reach. The two of us becoming what we are.

THE EVENING MEAL

Father folds up our house, puts it in his suitcase, then walks into the forest. When he arrives at the world's edge, he turns, pulls up the road, cracks it once like a whip, then slips it into his suitcase. Then he folds up the night.

"I'm going now," he says, and leaves.

I point to where our house once was, to where the road once was. I point to where there once was night.

"Sit," mother says and we sit.

We are a tiny family. We have small bones. We pull them out from inside our skin and pile them on the table. We place our serviettes on our miniscule laps, some of us first wiping the corners of our mouths, and the evening meal begins.

DOORBELL

This is an old picture of my two sons. Their pants are down and they are squatting. It looks like they are aligned with imaginary hole-in-the-ground toilets but my wife reminds me they were actually trying to give birth.

Did they become the three and five year-old fathers of tiny humans?

They spoke of people who lived behind our house, of what signs to look for and what to say in greeting. They built twig and leaf amusement parks.

Later, my eldest son dreamed the doctors under the sink had installed a doorbell in his bum. My other son told me he had swallowed an open window. The same window, he said, through which, a long time ago, tiny human children had crept in from outside and removed his wings, then replaced them with arms.

LIVING ROOM

I build a giant mountain in the centre of my living room. My wife and children climb it. I fall asleep on the couch, my white lotus-coloured belly hidden beneath a ratty MY OTHER ABS ARE A SIX PACK T-shirt. The TV hums. Somewhere in back, grandmother stirs the electronics and laughs.

I dream the world and it goes on forever. I dream of other fathers waking then drowning on their couches. I dream my wife safe from cancer: birds nibble her ears, build nests from her skin, feed their babies and teach them flying. A single egg neglects to hatch. It is huge. Inside, something sloshes around, trying to be one thing or another. Shadow fingers make dogs of light. My children find the world in a forgotten toybox covered with ants.

We are not alone, I say to the toybox, my words echoing deep inside the tunnels of my children's ears, my mouth itself a tunnel or the empty hands of an egg.

PIANO

My children asleep, I imagine a beard on the piano so it can be shaved. I put my hand in the wall, find the raisin between this world and its black rest.

This is the middle ages, not what came before, not what's next

MILK IN RAINDROPS

They throw the TV into the fire. Shadows flicker over cave walls. On the screen, a small heaven crenelated by flame.

They plug the TV into a mammoth. A mammoth appears on screen. They pull the plug and stick it into the river. The rush of water, floating leaves, logs realized later to be creatures engulfed by waves.

They plug the TV into itself. Nothing, then it appears on screen, frightened, meek, wanting home.

A ceremony. They marry the TV and it broadcasts them, the russet of sun, the purple sky, their words about life together. Children, remember our ancestors. Wisps, warnings, what's yet to be seen. A pillow, a mountain, the sound of leaves.

Night. The moon slithers, wary of ferns. The TV speaks, a hiss like embers in the fire. The slither and sibilance of its tongue, the slow static of birds, a tree of eyes. We believe babies find milk in raindrops, gather berries from the fields' thighs. We feast on mammoth light, the trace of hands, the stories that trust us.

DENTISTRY

Walk: this small chamber a mouth cleaned with precision. Rest: this reclining pulpit shines a light into your empty centre for we are bodies formed around empty space, the spelunking of throats, an astrophysics of breath and bite.

Recumbent celebrant, you expect a fridge, blender, or night train to rest on the tongue, pushing against teeth. Here the moon is soft and small, and slides between your lips. A train is coming. Now place this chair in your mouth. I will remove flowers, teeth, rabbits, decay and pain. I will inscribe, excise, scar, or circumcise. I will stalagmite and tattoo through a ceremony of implements and mirrors, I will perform elemental cybernetics, a chiselling of tusks. I will place things inside as pataphysical jokes: tubes, hoses, hands, butterscotch, metals, liquids, air. You will be frisked by fingers you cannot see. Breathe.

Now bite. Your mouth has no other light. It is a heraldry of teeth and it is sleep. It is a familiar, the shadow inside. Sleep is a slow motion practical joke, a dentistry of moon. Spit.

Now the bright sun. Now the face in the wind. Now the possibility of love, rain, starlings. Red tunnel. Russian dancers. Stairs. The thousand teeth of monkeys chattering waxed floss, alveolar ridge, and the procession of an orthodontic optimism in the future. Open your mouth to the world. Our work is done.

FENCING

after a collaboration with Victor Coleman

We had been whitewashing the fence that we'd been sitting on and were waiting for the paint to dry, watching it as if it were serious French cinema on an unengaging afternoon.

"French cinema is the breath of God, all filmy on the feathered behind-backs of the seraph serving," I said and the others laughed.

George raised his right eyebrow dryly. "I prefer to keep God at alms length," he said, and we chuckled, imagining we had all the time in the world.

Charlie discovered a few drips of paint on the fence. "It's as if a uvula in the cave of God's maw had become protean, proving that the vibrant proto-plasm of language is but a virus from author space." We drew in our breaths preparing to laugh drolly, but Henry, who was an angel, screeched up in his car, and we exhaled without laughing.

"Sorry I'm late. Heatstroke, you know—being an angel I have to keep everything—heater included—on high. But seriously, I was crooning down the road toward utter and prayer. I'd turned at the corner of divine interven-tion, at the border between the letter and the enveloped, and, if you can believe it, I was epistle whipped again. Here, let me read it to you."

We were all ears and wings and Henry began:

> "There once was a shoe salesman Elijah
> Who said I'd be happy to oblijah
> When your foot's neatly shod
> In the raiment of God
> In fear angels shall ne'er tread besidejah."

"It's a harp attack," I said, "in a region legion with Dionysian fission."

George moved his eyebrows around again. "It's a frisson allied with the anomaly," he said.

"Wish we were really human," I said.

"Yes," everyone agreed, and we waited by the fence for another five hundred thousand years.

SNUG

Outside my head, a great storm, dark, and the air snorts buffalo and doom. Clouds gather in furrows, the sky tosses with a doozer of a headache. Any picnics are not happy: the sandwiches are soggy, the Kool Aid's dilute, and everyone's irritated with father for continuing to state that, "It's all about being together," and, "It's attitude not details which determine success."

But look! A little sparrow swimming through the downpour. Doused, it's a flag in a hurricane. Whipped and tossed it finds an opening, a safe passage, a cave of respite. OK, my ear. It funnels deep into my cochlea. Finally a pink snail, some promise of satisfaction in the darkness. It keeps going, finding safe harbour in the snug of my brain. Now it's a feathery bumper car in the warm labyrinth of my fulgent mind. There's an image of my parents purchasing a new hose, my sister falling from a tree, and my grandpa's heart, clip-clopping like a pony inside the cobbles of his chest.

And still the sparrow flies through the shed of my skull, past the toolbox, the pitchfork, the medulla oblongata and that dream where my son gives birth to BB King and a window. An acorn licks a tree and the forest shudders. Then the bird heads south and emerges from the star of my anus, only to be lost to storm and uncertain darkness. I'm able to sit down—eventually—able to overcome fear and a memory of feathers.

"What comes before or after we do not know," my father says, sucking on a damp sandwich. "Only the bird's short flight, the dog's incessant yip, the shelf that shines when the storm is outside."

BRICK

An entire wall of brick but only this one brick inside me, a brick for my labyrinth of blood, of glowering and sadness. The brick is the sky. A herd of bees. The brick is seven sheep wandering across my chest in the terra cotta morning. The edges of the brick, its corners. Flesh of my brick. Here we are at this wall and our world is filled with bricks. Our cell walls, our tongue walls, the walls of our dogs. This brick. We haven't yet been born.

DUSK. DUST. NIGHT. DAY. KNIFE.

Of course we don't know where he is, Raoul Wallenberg gave himself another passport, became someone else, then disappeared. A curled brown leaf.

He spoke as they were about to board, gave each word a new identity. Now we don't know what they mean. A long ditch running beside the road. Home.

Over there, behind the moon. Behind words. Fingers intertwined, churning like a river mill, sun climbing the horizon, rising over the field. A scurrying in twilight. A woolen blanket folded over and over. Eight times the limit of folding. Then it disappears, was never there.

Transfuse my veins with sap, fill a tree with blood. Branches move slowly in a slow wind. Autumn at the end of the fingers, red, gold, brown. Curling. When I am made into boards, a chair, this floor. Dance on me. Hide underneath me. Hush. Listen. Owls.

Stories told by the bakehouse. Childbed. Midnight. A mandolin. In another's skin, a wolf creeping through mountains carrying only flour, an extra hand in a basket. Blood drains through the wicker.

Moonlight, silver tongue, wolf spine. The shine of a wrist, sneaking through fields and they in their grey uniforms, hissing, pointing guns, not knowing. Inside the baked loaf, a passport, money, an eyeball.

Names filtered through trees. Seven layers of clothing. Skirt. Shirt. Coat. Shirt. Pelt. Leaves. Bark. Dress. Shirt. Dusk. Dust. Night. Day. Knife. Stars. Hush. A shoe busy with insects. A morsel fingered in a pocket. A new planet. Backwards and forwards. Sleep.

Night is a length of a train, morning shuddering down the days, drifting smoke. Razors and breath hidden in lapels, rabbit skins, an unshaven face. Father cigarette. A hidden cave. Mother eyelid. The city folded eight times and bound by streets. Under the corn, sky roads. What they don't know: leaves have our names.

Blackbirds an almost remembered song. Oxen, cobblestones. The heart heals the knife, old potato. You fold and refold the words but they don't disappear. A river forming over time or through memory, but less wet.

The moon is samovar, ship, the galaxy smear of light spangled against a Baltic blue sky Shh. He writes his own passport. We don't know what it means.

Clouds and rivers. A torn newspaper photo with no face. A passport above the desk. A Vienna of beds. A Vilnius. When you cease to be who you are, you don't become someone else.

THE NEW SQUEEZE

A new accordion because the accordion is the world and it should do more than push and pull. The hiss and sigh, the 1 and 0, the squeeze and press are three dimensions only, considering time. But what of Newton's up and down, sink and rise, backward and forward, away and toward, what of the new tessitura of spacetime, the infolding diapason within the electron, the asymptotic passacaglias of hadrons, the tiny cassotto of exotic mesons and tetraquarks? There's a cave filled with the shadows of accordions or of accordion music. There's a pyre of accordions alight. We cannot know if the accordion plays or not, or is inflamed, or both. The caged accordion observed is not the incorporeal accordion true. An accordion may be dimensionless polka or a chatroom hora, but we cannot know if it is Mozart, if its shadows play the numinous ompah of root and fifth, if our true love wrapped in an accordion is but an emergent system of grace notes and obligatos drawn from our connected minds, or stripped naked to the waist, what risk is ours to play. Inside the accordion, the vast multidimensional darkness of the possible; above us, the constellation of buttons and keys, the dance pattern of what we know already and would now like to forget.

WITHOUT BLINKING

North, south, east, west. Giantess has four eyes.

They walk the hill. "The mountains, the ocean, the mountains, the ocean." They hear starlings in the sky, grass beneath wind.

"Bake," they say but don't have to say because they already know, joined at the mind.

"Cake," they say, and return to the kitchen to mix, their hands a blur, their smiles, crinkled eyes, their mouths taking sweet cake within the hour. A warm rolling happiness through shared regions.

And they look at the plate, the pantry, the window and through the door. They look north, west, east, south. They move through the world like it surrounds them.

They have babies. Giantess has babies. Each a warm rolling happiness that grew in the red thicket of their middle. Four babies, individual, mewling, sputtering, learning to speak with joy, recognition, disquiet, or love. And Giantess picks up their babies and props them on their hips, holds them in their forest of arms, feeds them from their flock of breasts. The babies sleep, are covered with blankets knit with lambs and ears, clouds and trees. They sigh, the babies and the Giantess.

Through their eyes they look at their babies. And at the room behind their babies. And through the windows and the door beside their babies and hear the townspeople coming and they stand at the door. They stand at the door with their axes in their several arms and the townspeople marching with their axes and their many chants of "We will divide you or the blood of your several circulations will wet the green grass."

Giantess at the door waits for the townspeople, their babies individual and sleeping in the crib, axes held by their hips. Giantess waiting.

4.

THE SAXOPHONISTS' BOOK OF THE DEAD

As soon as Miss Billie Holiday turned to write on the blackboard, Lester Young whipped out his peashooter and fired a spitball right where she had written the date. The spitball rolled down into the chalk gutter, leaving a damp opalescent trail.

"Pfft," Coleman Hawkins said, shaking his head at Lester. Before Miss Holiday turned around—she first finished writing the double bar at the end of the song—Hawk shot another spitball right at her butt. There was a rippling around the point of impact on her sleek, dark skirt.

"John Coltrane," she said looking at me. "John William Coltrane. I know you helped pioneer the use of modes in jazz and later were at the forefront of free jazz. I know you were recognized for your masterful improvisation, supreme musicianship and iconic centrality to the history of jazz, but you march yourself down to Principal Hodges' office right now and I don't mean later."

"Yes, Miss Holiday," I said, standing. Ben Webster looked back from the seat in front of me and mouthed Miss Holiday's words as soon as she said them, opening his mouth wide like a satchel.

I wasn't worried about the principal's office. I'd been there before. My buddy Bird had taught me to play "Cherokee" in at least twenty-one keys. I could handle the principal. Before long we'd be talking about his lifetime in the Ellington band, about Harry Carney, and even about Billy Strayhorn and Mercer. And besides, what was he going to do, send me home? We all knew there was nothing beyond the classroom. At the end of the school's linoleum, things just faded out. Nothing but the empty sky of infinite space and the chorus of stars.

I walked out of the classroom but stood for a moment outside the door, listening as Miss Holiday continued the lesson. We were learning "All the Things You Are," even though we'd all played the song a thousand times.

"Who can tell me what happens during the bridge?" she asked.

Eric Dolphy's hand shot into the air. This should be good, I thought. Eric was always pushing things right to the edge.

"Yes, Eric?" Miss Holiday said. There was something about Miss Holiday's voice that was so fragile yet still kept us in our place. Even Lester. At recess, he would defend her when the other boys began to talk. And I wondered if he deliberately missed when he shot his spitballs. He'd get that crazy look in his eyes, twist his head funny, and shoot the peashooter at a weird angle and never get it anywhere near her. Still, a river of saliva down the board was something. Most guys, the spitball would just bounce and land on the floor with only a small dab of wet where it had hit. And there were those times when Lester would play a song with Miss Holiday. Even though his conception of rhythm and harmony were rudimentary compared to the sophistication that I felt I'd achieved, especially in my later years. I couldn't help but feel moved in a sleepy, old-timey kind of way.

"Miss Holiday," Eric began. "You know where the G-sharp melody note over the E major chord turns into an A-flat over the F minor seventh at the turnaround of the B section?"

"Yes, Eric," Miss Holiday said. "But please stand when you speak in class."

"Sorry, Miss Holiday," he said, shuffling to his feet. "In my estimation that's a particularly striking employment of an enharmonic substitution in an American popular song, and one that facilitates the use of a chord built on every one of the twelve tones of the chromatic scale."

"That's an astute observation, Eric. And one that reflects your particular sensitivity to heightened chromaticism, something that is often tragically mis-understood. You may sit down."

"Thank you, Miss Holiday," he said. I couldn't tell if Eric had been trying to be sarcastic. Sometimes he was very subtle. But Miss Holiday had handled him deftly, I thought.

Out of nowhere, Lester suddenly murmured, "You are the angel glow."

"Pardon me?" Miss Holiday said. "YATAG, ma'am." It was Charlie Parker, slouched as always in the back row, his nose stuck deep in a book as if he wasn't listening.

"YATAG. 'You are the angel glow.' Some of the most beautiful lyrics of all time. In the B section, ma'am."

My own favourite line was, "What did I long for? I never really knew." It was in the verse, which was almost never sung.

I started walking to Principal Hodges' office. Deep space loomed at the end of the hall, just past the pictures of the student council and the pop machine. A rich velvet darkness and the stage lights of the silver stars.

The door was half open and I could see Principal Hodges in his customary ash-coloured wide-lapelled suit, chair tilted back, shiny shoes up on the desk, his eyes barely open, a haze of smoke like an interstellar dust cloud settled around him.

"Time and again I've longed for adventure, 'Something to make my heart beat the faster'," he said through the door. "John William Coltrane...Trane," he said, motioning for me to enter. "How long have we known each other?" he asked.

"A thousand years, sir," I replied, though I didn't really know how long, having little to measure it by.

"And here you are at my office again? I thought we'd developed an under-standing."

"It wasn't me, sir. It was Coleman," I said.

"That's what you told me the last time. And before that, you said it was Lester." He took a long drag on his cigarette and then blew it out in an extended blue sigh. "John," he said. "John, it's about listening. The others look up to you. It's time to take responsibility."

"Yes, sir," I said, looking at the floor, the many burn marks like dark constellations in the taupe linoleum tiles. "Responsibility."

"Now go back to class and do what's right."

"Yes, sir," I nodded.

"Can you really play 'Cherokee' in all twelve keys?"

"Yes, sir. Charlie taught me. And it's at least twenty-one if you consider the enharmonic spellings."

"Right," he said. "But they don't sound any different, do they?"

"No, sir."

"Before you return to class, John, I would like you to take a long walk around the school and think about what I've said."

"Yes, Principal Hodges," I said, knowing that what he asked was impossible, that I'd be lost in empty space like all the others.

I went back down the hall and listened again at the classroom door.

I heard the click of cases opening, a small thrumming of fingers on saxophone keys as my classmates held reeds in their mouths, saturating them with spit to prepare them for playing. I heard the small talk, the muttered jokes, the first few riffs, and the plangent vibrato of high notes. The quick whistle, the resultant shout as someone hit someone else with a spitball when they weren't looking.

I went back into the classroom.

"O.K.," Miss Holiday said. "John's back. Get your tenor out, John, and let's take it from the top."

THE LONG WAY HOME

After wearing it a few times, the dog got used to the muzzle and stopped trying to paw it off. In fact, when Vent took it down from the coat hook, the dog became excited, because, along with the plastic poop-and-scoop bag, Vent's boots, and the leash, the dog now associated it with the walks they took at midnight, when Vent's wife and kids were sleeping, folding laundry, preparing for work, or talking online with their friends. Two weeks ago, Vent had had a meaningless lump removed from his mouth. How much of ourselves don't we need? he wondered. What else could they have thrown over the edge of the operating table as unwanted ballast?

It was 12:30 and Vent was walking the dog across the soccer fields by the highway, a strong wind making the April night cool. The almost full moon shone off the dog's white fur and the muzzle glinted silver over the dark green grass. The dog in relation to the moon as the moon to the sun. Hundreds of years ago, Vent mused, his hallucinations would have made him a visionary or a madman, dreaming while awake, seeing visions from shadows, spectres in the moonlight, ghosts at midday. Hundreds of years ago, he'd not have been mildly walking through the night holding a blue plastic leash and a plastic shopping bag for dogshit. When was the first time someone walked a dog on a leash? When was the first time someone had a lump removed? When was the first time someone had their dog's teeth cleaned professionally?

There were train tracks at the end of the field, and on the other side of them, a remote part of the old city graveyard below the hill. The wire fence in front of the tracks was cut open and bent back to form a gate. Vent went through and crossed the tracks and into the field of gravestones, some leaning forward, some back, some fallen over. An orthodontist would feel the excitation of a big job to be done here. Imagine a second set of permanent gravestones pushing up, pushing out the baby stones. Of course, everyone thought of gravestones as teeth. The empty grave like the hole left by an extracted molar, worried by the tongue until it healed. Vent could feel his throat healing, the scarring over, the sensitive tissue inaccessible, his throat something like an empty grave. It'd taken about a week before he could eat regular foods, before his diet of ice cream, smoothies, and soups could expand once again to include solids.

There was a bench by a twisted tree and Vent sat down. The dog twitched a bit, hearing something on the wind, the muzzle lit by the canteloupe-coloured light of the streetlamp. What would it be like to wear the muzzle? Would it be like a football facemask or the helm of a knight? On impulse, he undid the leather straps and fitted them over his ears, the muzzle hanging heavy from his nose and chin. The dog looked quizzically, wondering how this new communication fit into the idea of walk. Vent felt the raw hollowness of his throat, felt the leather pulling at his ears, adjusted the strap that attached over the middle of his head. He took off the dog's collar and put it around his own neck. He attached the leash and held it out. The dog took it in its mouth and began walking. Vent followed, bending down to maintain the slackness of the leash. They went down a winding path which led around some pine trees and a storage shed. A mausoleum in grainy lichen-covered marble. The wind sighed over the trees at the top of the hill. Vent and the dog walking. The full clouds were a vivid chiaroscuro as the moon passed between them. There was the sound of a firetruck, siren keening, horn braying. The dog stopped at a stone marker. It seemed very old and indicated a particular section of the graveyard. The dog lifted its leg and began to urinate, an impossibly long and steady stream dribbling down the side of the marker and forming a small pool at its base. Vent shifted uphill somewhat to avoid the runoff. Then Vent and the dog proceeded.

He had two children. A boy of sixteen and a girl of twelve. Just this morning, his daughter had had her first period and had gone running to his wife with the news. She was excited to have arrived at this important moment, one she'd been waiting for, talking about with her mother. His son, Vincent, had his own world of skateboarding, friends bucking the system by wearing oversized and overbranded skateboard-themed clothing. Vent had a close, if not especially talkative, relationship with his children. The same, in fact, could be said about his relations with his wife.

It was now about 1:30 and the dog had led Vent through the newer parts of the cemetery. The gravestones were smoother, the engraving more precise. Some had chosen a more modern approach: a large cube balanced, as if for eternity, on one of its vertices, gravestones in the shape of parallelograms with stylish sans serif inscriptions, shiny black marble with grey lettering and embedded blue glass.

What if I never trade back places with the dog? Vent thought.

They had left the graveyard and were walking back over the high-level bridge and past the former Governor General's house and the small hotel where Vent had once, as a student, attended an information session about selling encyclopedias. It was a 'tremendous opportunity for a bright and energetic person to share learning with others door to door.' They were walking toward the plaza just past the gas station and the highway entrance, the plaza which contained the grocery store, the sub shop and the place where they bought the dog's kibble.

The dog, Vent realized, was taking the long way home.

TART. SWEET. CRUNCHY. CRISP.

We were sitting in a waiting room outside the big office. I'd brought a copy of a jazz magazine to read and it sat on my lap, unopened. She was around my age, mid-twenties, her dark hair tied back, her jeans and T-shirt plain and nondescript. Did you know that Chet Baker died by falling out of a window? she asked. Imagine, she said, the propped window, Chet's lank body draped sideways over the sill, a leg dangling over the edge as he gazes out at the Amsterdam street below. He's singing a tune in his sweet voice. Maybe it's "When I Fall in Love," because then he really did fall.

It might have been an accident, she said. Yes, there was heroin in his system and cocaine in the hotel room. So that might have had something to do with it. It wasn't likely murder because the door was locked from the inside. And a window only two storeys up wouldn't be a good choice to jump from, don't you think? He was kind of a worn-out angel, but he was making some of the best records of his career. Then he pulped his head on the concrete. He already didn't have teeth and had had to learn to play trumpet all over again, except with dentures. After the fall, he couldn't very well play without a head. Though I suppose a few have tried, she laughed sweetly. And then added, suddenly serious, We lose people like that. Without warning.

We'd been sitting for a couple of hours in the small waiting area, just a few chairs, a couple of worn magazines, and some kind of batiked fabric art from the seventies. I knew there was something I should have said when she became serious, but I hesitated, not knowing what, and then it was too late. I'd taken too long.

I thought of it later. Sponsor me in the gravity-a-thon. Sponsor me in the grav-
ity-a-thon today, for I will remain pulled to the earth forever. You can sponsor me
by the hour or the day. You can pay in one lump sum, which, considering my mass
and shape, might be most appropriate. I will help hold things together. I will be
pulled toward the centre of many things and this pulling will help. Things will stay
together. They will remain clumped, pressed down like soil in the path of wide-
hooved horses. The roads of the world shall not erode, and its mountains will not fly
through the clouds.

But I too have my own force in the universe. I pull matter toward me. The sun.
Jupiter. A raisin. Galaxies and superclusters. Gnats. There is attraction. Far from
home, the shape of a comet, and its path changes because of me. Even more if I eat
this next sandwich or that apple.

And there is an attraction that flows between the stuff of everything. The citizens
of the world, its fish, and its stones. Gravity flows between us like an aura that
shakes hands, that clasps us together as a drowning swimmer and his rescuer tug at
each other over the edge of the boat, as waves rise and fall, escaping from the ocean
and returning, escaping and returning, as indeed the moon pulls the tides, a restless
sleeper tugging on blankets, pulled by dreams.

And I will sponsor you also. I will sponsor you and you will sponsor me. We both
will move toward the centre of the world. I will pull you toward me and you will
pull back. We will pull the living and the dead toward us. We are swimmers in an
ocean of tide and undertow, an ocean of time and space.

But, of course, it would have been typical of me to think of that. I'd have
wanted to stand up in my superhero cape in the waiting room and make
everything right, speaking not for the meaning, but for how the words fell on
the tongue. Still, though, the sudden seriousness of her words stayed with me:
We lose people like that. The words like a plaintive hole in space, like someone
had erased a shadow, leaving nothing, not even the air.

I saw her again about a month later, walking down the stairs to the big office.

Hi, I said awkwardly. Do you know which jazz composer has a middle name that's a shape?

I don't know, Benny Square Goodman? she said with a scrunching of her right eye, like a kind of wink.

Actually, it was Melodious Thunk, I said.

Who?

Thelonious Monk—his middle name was Sphere.

The opposite of square, she said. His own planet.

Yes, I said. But they always say his music is so angular.

O.K. then, a planet with lots of feet and elbows sticking out of it.

That's some kind of strange gravity happening there.

I guess, she said. And then was gone.

I continued up the stairs and sat down in the waiting room. After an hour or so, the door to the big office opened and I was asked to come in to another smaller waiting room, though with similar decor. There was a clipboard on the table beside my chair. There were forms to fill out, and I began. My name, my age, the town where I was born. The story of my childhood. My mother's maiden name. Grades I got in college. I wrote about apples that I liked at different times in my life. Tart. Sweet. Crunchy. Crisp. My first bicycle. What dental work I needed. My job, my investments, my new car. Retirement plans and the last tropical country I travelled to. And as I wrote, I remained fixed to my place in the chair. I was balanced perfectly between one thing and the next. I had gravity and there was gravity, but I did not fall.

THE NARROW SEA

There was an accident and the truck overturned. Some were confused, suffering shock and head injuries and they began to wander aimlessly along the road. The rest of us made for the neighbourhoods. We climbed fences and took exit ramps. We walked the crescents and courts of the subdivisions. We stepped past the rolled up newspapers and the discount store flyers, saw the sweet green grass sticking through the melting snow and so walked toward the lawns. People were told to stay away from the windows so that we weren't spooked. We saw them looking away from their televisions, peering from the corners of windows. We were mortal ghosts tarrying in their yards but we were not afraid.

"Mrs. Brimby," I said to the cow next to me. "Do you remember?"

"Yes," Mrs. Brimby said. "I remember."

Then there was shouting. Humans in uniform with ropes and guns, and hoops on the end of long poles.

They didn't see us as we slipped behind a triple-car garage and into the lane behind a convenience store. We waited between the blue dumpster and the wall.

Finally, night fell and the air became cool, the only sound, the nearby highway like the exhalations of the sea.

The moon set and we left our hiding place.

We came across two youths wheeling a folded ping-pong table down the middle of the road. We nodded at each other, complicit in our secret tasks, and kept going.

By the highway, the service road was empty, the weeds of its rising embankments offering us cover. We had only a few hours before sunrise.

"What do you think happened to the others?" I asked.

"They panicked," Mrs. Brimby said.

There was a young man on the top of the embankment. "I'm going to catch you," he shouted.

I felt sorry for him.

"Come with us," I said.

"No, you must come with me," he said.

We stood in front of him, the moon casting our shadows together like a dark puddle.

We waited.

He knew it was futile. We were two large animals and he was a spindly youth. He lowered his stick.

"I have something to show you," he said, finally.

His name was Mike. He was working for the summer with Animal Control while he attended college. He had stayed out late, far beyond the end of his shift, in the hope of doing something marvellous, of finding us, of impressing his superiors. His new girlfriend, from the city, also worked with animals and he called her on his cell phone. He listened intently to her instructions.

He led us along the service road, across a main street bright with gas stations and fast-food restaurants, and down a long multi-lane boulevard. His girlfriend, Rose, arrived. She was bright and fresh-looking and held out her hand in greeting when she got out of her car, then smiled at the absurdity of the gesture, and changed it into a little wave.

Mike helped Rose take something out of the trunk. They began pulling it up around themselves.

A cow costume.

Rose, who was the front end, gestured with her nose.

"What should we do?" I asked Mrs. Brimby.

"Follow them," she said.

We passed under a gateway and through some well-manicured gardens. We walked around a large glass building and stopped at a side door. Rose reached out from the abdomen of the costume and opened it with a key.

We shuffled along a concrete corridor, then down a few stairs. There was a vast glass wall, the window of a huge tank. Inside, the water was luminous. Enormous creatures, whales of some kind, sailed around the bright blue fields singing their bittersweet song.

The three of us, two cows and two humans, watched through the glass as dawn came in through the high windows.

"The ocean," I said.

"Yes," said Mrs. Brimby, "I remember."

PHIL CAMPBELL WAS HIS TOWN

There's a guy called Phil Campbell who lives in a town in Alabama called Phil Campbell. It was exhausting: the questions, the confusion, the wisecracks:

"So you're Phil Campbell and you live in Phil Campbell...?"

Phil Campbell thought about moving, thought about changing his name, but he never did. Phil Campbell was his home. It was his name. He was Phil Campbell and Phil Campbell was his town.

But Phil Campbell wasn't named after Phil Campbell, the town. He was named Phil Campbell after his father, Phil Campbell. And this Phil Campbell had been named after his own father, Phil Campbell, who had been named after his father, a stocky and redoubtable man named Phil Campbell. But that's as far as it went, for that Phil Campbell was the progeny of George Campbell, a migrant who had moved to Phil Campbell from somewhere up north, no one was sure where. On the other hand, Phil Campbell, the town, was named in the 1880s after a railroad man named Phil Campbell who came from England and set up a work camp. The town was incorporated in 1911 and remains the only place in Alabama to have both a first and a last name.

"Hey, Phil Campbell, you come from Phil Campbell?"

"That's *Mister* Phil Campbell to you."

It was a good life in Phil Campbell. Safe streets, good jobs, a good digestion and a smooth complexion. A happy life.

But this past April, a tornado ripped through Phil Campbell and messed things up. Here's what happened.

Bricks, windows, record collections, small chairs from the elementary school, fridges, bank deposits, Phil Campbells' pants, cows: all tossed into the air and then scattered over the hot Alabama ground. A toupée was blown, forlorn and alone down Main Street, baleful tumbleweed, inventory spat from the twisting chaos of the air. There were tears flying horizontally like rain. There were small bursts of hope, but there was little to hope for.

Phil Campbell would never be the same.

He'd been working in his basement for days and hadn't got the tornado warnings. He'd come up to the kitchen to get himself a glass of orange juice when he heard strange sounds outside and so he opened the door to see what was going on. The tornado burst right through the door. And when Phil Campbell opened his mouth to say, "Hey, what do you think you're …?" the tornado jumped in. Phil Campbell's insides became as messed up as the streets of the town, and he fell down and lay on the clammy linoleum beside the stove and passed out.

That's where the other Phil Campbells enter the story. One thousand one hundred and fifty Phil Campbells. Phil Campbells from all around the world.

These Phil Campbells found each other on Facebook, through Twitter, and through regular email. They gathered in the town of Phil Campbell. They came to see what they could do.

Philanthropy.

It was mostly guys named Philip and a few Phyllises, though there were Phillipas and Filipes, too. They all wore nametags. Identical nametags, photocopied by Phil Campbell of Phil Campbell Real Estate (Boston, Mass.)

"Phil Campbell," the nametags said, both with irony and without.

It was a serious thing, this meeting of Phil Campbells, but it was droll pandemonium when they registered at the hotel.

"I've a reservation under the name Phil Campbell," a Phil Campbell would say at the Phil Campbell Motor Inn and the other Phil Campbells in the line behind him laughed good-naturedly at the confusion of the girl at the desk.

And there were the many Phil jokes.

"Hey Phil," a Phil would call into the whole group of Phils just to see who would turn around.

Or the ever popular, "Philately will get you nowhere."

"I've had my Phil," a Phil Campbell father would quip about his son, another Phil Campbell.

And there were murmurs of assent as a Phil Campbell patted his handsome round Campbell-belly and ordered a Philly Cheese Steak sandwich at the Phil Campbell Steakhouse with the words, "I need a Phil-up, please."

But no matter how you looked at it—joyfully, wryly, bizarrely, wonderfully—there were a lot of Phils.

"Hey Phil, where are you from?" one Phil would ask another.

"Brooklyn. Where you from?"

"Toronto, Canada," the first Phil would reply.

Groups of Phil Campbells sat together and talked. There wasn't anything special about being Phil Campbell if you lived in a place other than Phil Campbell, in Seattle or Liverpool or Prague, for instance. There weren't special Phil Campbell stories, the way someone who shared a name with a famous celebrity had stories.

"You're Flip Philips?"

"Not *that* Flip Philips."

"Oh, but please, have a seat in First Class and may I have your autograph? For my kids."

But being Phil Campbell became remarkable when you were in a group of over a thousand other Phil Campbells.

"One can of beans isn't special, but if you see a thousand cans of beans lined up in a row, then that's something," a Phil Campbell from Hoboken, New Jersey explained to a Phil Campbell from Tucson, Arizona.

And being with one thousand one hundred and forty-nine other Phil

Campbells in the Phil Campbell Catering and Banquet Center in Phil Campbell, Alabama was not just unusual enough to make a good story. It was sublime.

An alignment of electrons. A ringing harmony, a magnetic charge.

What was the same? What was different? What's it like where you come from? How did you hear about the town of Phil Campbell?

But then the Phil Campbells turned to the more serious matter at hand. "How can all of us Phil Campbells help the people of Phil Campbell?" The tornado had been bad. People had been killed. Many were missing. Phil Campbell was filled with debris. There were emergency rescue crews, but they were overwhelmed.

The Phil Campbells made plans. They would tend to the sick and traumatized, search for the missing. They would clean up, help rebuild, and assist people in finding new homes. Each Phil Campbell according to his or her own skills, profession, and nature, and resources. There were Officer Phils, Nurse Phils, Construction-worker Phils, and, of course, several Dr. Phils.

They set to work.

With spades and wheelbarrows, pick-up trucks and bandages.

With kindness, determination, and goofy grins.

Army cots were set up in the high school gym. Enormous pots of soup were set to boil in the kitchens of churches. An infirmary ran out of the flagship Phil Campbell Pizza Emporium. A team of Phils began going door-to-door—or property-to-property when the doors or the houses had been knocked down—searching for those in need. Old men and women were helped outside, blinking in the bright light, as if emerging from a cave, and then driven to the gym. Mothers and their small children were lifted off their broken porches and taken for food at Phil Campbell Baptist Church.

"How you doing, Phil Campbell?" one Phil would ask another.

"Doing fine, thank you, Phil Campbell," the other would reply and they'd both smile. Two Phil Campbells out in the world, doing good.

"OK," one of them said into the crackling walkie-talkie. "Just going to check one more street before heading back for more supplies."

Phil Campbell's street hadn't been hit hard. Really, it looked almost untouched. The lawns, neatly manicured, the shingles in place on the roofs, only garbage pails and flowerpots tossed about the sidewalks. Still, the team of Phil Campbells went up and down the street, checking each house just to make sure.

Phil Campbell's door was open.

"Hello, anyone here?" they called.

No answer.

Phil Campbell was still unconscious on the floor, his bald head in a pool of almost evaporated orange juice sticky between the shards of broken glass scattered over the linoleum. The Phil Campbells moved quickly. One checked for a pulse. The other brushed the glass out of the way to make a clear workspace and then prepared the medical kit and held up the walkie-talkie, ready to call for outside help.

"He's alive," the first Phil Campbell said. He took a small flashlight from his pocket, pulled up Phil Campbell's eyelid, and shone the light at his pupil. "Responsive," he said.

"Sir?" he called to Phil Campbell. "Can you hear me?" He leaned in close to listen to Phil Campbell's breathing. "Help me," he said to the other Phil Campbell. "Let's sit him up." One Phil Campbell supported his head and they pulled Phil Campbell up and rested him against the cabinet doors below the sink.

Phil Campbell began to breathe heavily and his eyes fluttered.

"What's your name, sir?" the second Phil Campbell asked. "Do you know your name?"

"Ph...Ph...Phil Campbell," Phil Campbell said weakly.

"That's *my* name," the Phil Campbell who had supported his neck said. "It's all of our names."

"Phil Campbell," Phil Campbell repeated. "I am Phil Campbell."

"Yes, sir," Phil Campbell said. "Your name is Phil Campbell. It's our name, too."

Phil Campbell opened his mouth to say something more, but he could not contain the tornado any longer and it turned violently inside him and shot from the cave of his throat. It knocked both Phil Campbells down as it twisted about the kitchen and then burst out of the house with an ear-splitting howl.

It beat against the houses and trees of Phil Campbell's street, this time smashing and scattering everything in its seemingly erratic path toward the centre of town. It destroyed the elementary school and knocked down the library. It raged along the side streets and ripped through the mall.

One of the Phil Campbells, rolled over on his belly and reached for the walkie-talkie. He must alert the other Phil Campbells.

Later that afternoon, there were one thousand one hundred and fifty-one Phil Campbells gathered together on Main St. They stood in a line on the other side of the street from the tornado. It seethed and spun in place like a tied-up bull at a rodeo.

Phil Campbell, the only Phil Campbell from Phil Campbell, Alabama walked forward.

"My name is Phil Campbell," he said to the tornado. "You are powerful and you have ravaged my town. You have killed many of my people, but I am not afraid. You plunged inside me and messed my guts up. But I understand you now. I stand here with all of these other Phil Campbells. Phil Campbells who have come here from all over the world. These Phil Campbells are not afraid either."

The tornado turned and twisted and darkened the sky but did not move.

Phil Campbell bent down and picked up the lost toupée from the middle of the street. Though it was dusty and misshapen, he put it on his bald head.

"You know what I'm going to call you?" Phil Campbell said to the tornado. "I'm going to call you, Phil Campbell. You're one of us now."

And just as the tornado had been inside him, he stepped into the tornado, into its empty insides.

The last time anyone saw Phil Campbell of Phil Campbell, Alabama, he was high in the air, holding onto the toupée and waving back at them from between the twisting fury of the tornado, just barely visible from the outside.

If the people of Phil Campbell could have named their town after Phil Campbell, they would have, but more than a hundred years before, they already had.

FATHERHOOD

Late night and we decide to have a son, the whole goddamn pack of us, standing outside the pool hall, quite young ourselves. We didn't exactly say it out loud, but a consensus is reached, decided, as these things usually are, through the mutual recognition of stirrings deep inside us, passed around without comment by a silent network.

And how does a group of us have a son? Sure there are methods. Girlfriends. Wives. We've thought about it. Or kidnap. But tonight, maybe it is the moon, or the combination of shooters and what is up our nose, but we stand outside the pool hall waiting, smoking, knowing something will happen. We don't have to do anything. It'll come to us.

A soft-faced boy walks out of the side door with a girl. He looks like us, except for the soft face. He isn't hiding it.

"Hey," we say. "We heard what you said to her. She's our friend."

"I didn't say anything."

"You sure as fuck did. You asked her for a hand-job, you fuck."

"I fucking did not. I was just asking about her baby."

"You fucking asked for a hand-job, dickhead."

"Did fucking not. We were in Grade 8 together. I was asking how she was."

"Fucking liar."

"Screw off, you dickwads. Fuck yourselves. I fucking said nothing."

And then we pull his jacket over his head and begin punching him until he falls down. We kick him with our twelve right feet, with a few left kicks mixed in for variety. He makes a bunch of sounds that aren't really words then rolls over to face the ground. We kick his head. End of Round 1.

Then he gets up. He isn't big but we can tell he works out.

"Fucking asshole."

He gets one of us right in the nose. Maybe all of us. Then again in the jaw. It's like a strike of lightning in the face. Everything dark except for the bright bolt where he connected. We get him in the side then connect with his teeth. A knee goes into his gut and his fist slams the side of a head. Two people fall to the ground. An ear and then a nose again. He has one of us by the hair, pulls the head up and then hard down against the pavement. Kaleidoscopes out both eyes and then all of us begin kicking him hard in the head, the legs, the gut. His nose bleeds, his teeth break. The moon pokes its face over the parking lot but it hides behind clouds, the fucking chicken. End of Round 2.

"OK, asshole. Round 3." He staggers to his feet again. We are in a circle now. "Ready to fight some more?" There are big welts over his forehead. One of his eyes is swollen shut. Some blood out the corner of his lip. He spits stuff from his mouth.

"Fucking round three. You too much of a pussy? Need your mommy and her tits?"

He walks away down the sidewalk.

"Pussy," we call after him. "Chickenshit."

So now we have a son. The whole goddamn pack of us. We're fathers. That's how it's done.

WALK TALL, CANNONBALL

for Nicholas Papaxanthos

We were playing chess online and talking, Charles and me.

Rook takes Knight. Check. Charles made some joke about the old jazz song, "Mercy, Mercy, Mercy."

I took the bait.

I asked, "So you like jazz?"

Knight takes Rook.

"Not until I lost my legs."

Queen takes pawn. Check.

I didn't know this guy, Charles—this was the first time we'd played together—but I went ahead and asked. "Lost your legs?" I said. "What happened?"

King takes Queen.

"It was during the war. Great nations were secretly blowing the world to pieces. Planes. Troops. Bombs. Enormous battleships patrolled the waters between continents and cut up the sea."

Bishop to Bishop 5. Double check.

"Sailors ran around inside the gun turrets, loaded charges and gunners shot brilliant saxophonists back and forth at each other, sometimes broadside, sometimes stoving in the galley or toppling the citadel."

King to King 1.

"Yes. It was another time, another world. A world where Cannonball Adderley was a weapon. A time of great adventure."

"And you lost your legs?"

"Early June. A battle near the African coast. Cannonball Adderley smashed across the foredeck and took me down with his blues-inflected post-bop. I woke up a week later in a hospital without legs. I didn't know what had happened. The bright morning sun. A light breeze rippling through white curtains. The green scent of trees. The nurse ran a damp cloth across my forehead. She was singing quietly. "Summertime, and the living is…"

"Where am I?" I asked.

"Shh." she said. "Fish are jumping." She pulled the blankets around me. "And the cotton is…" She walked quietly from the room.

I slept then, waking for small moments throughout the day, and then as day faded into night.

Darkness. Some sailor beside me coughing, then asking, "Anyone there?"

"Yeah," I said. "At least the part that's left." I wasn't certain of much, but I knew that. "Don't know where my legs are. In the ocean, maybe."

"Where are we now?" the sailor beside me asked.

"Some kind of hospital," I said.

"My name's Julian," the sailor said. "They call me Cannonball."

"Cannonball? As in Cannonball *Adderley*?"

"Yeah, like that. Used to eat a lot as a kid. 'Cannibal' my friends called me. Over time, it turned into 'Cannonball.' So did I. I was quite round, in fact."

"I didn't know then that he was the one who took off my legs. Just knew his name was the name of a great jazz musician. Anyway, it wasn't his choice: who would choose to be fired from a cannon? And besides, there were many Cannonballs in that war. Many Adderleys. The seas were full of dazzling jazz saxophonists, spent and sunk down to the sea floor.

"How you doing?" I said.

"Not good," he said. "Dizzy. Nauseous. Like I'm going to die. Or just did. And I don't know where my brother is. Nat. Nat Adderley. You know him?"

"Of course," I said. "The soulful brass salve to the incisive rippling edge of your alto's voluble spring."

"Yeah, that's him," he said. "But I'm worried. I haven't seen him since we were brought below deck. They lit him on fire, you know. He burned well. Hot and quick. Me, I was for smashing things. I destroyed rigging, stove in the sides of ships. I crashed through decks of men. And then, I would dance a nimble harmonic filigree, a razor-sharp hummingbird path around the changes of a jazz standard.

"All our lives, we looked after each other, though he was the younger brother. Spent all our time together ever since we were kids in Tampa. Playing ball on the sidewalk. Riding bikes to the beach. Piano lessons. Sword fighting. Nat and me, buying candy. Chess on the porch with grandpa, cake with grandma. Running from corner store bullies. Maybe doing some bullying ourselves. Down in the ravine, pouring a can of gasoline on the creek and lighting it on fire. But music. Always music. Four-handed piano. School pep band. Jazz. The church. Two brothers joined by blood and sound."

He coughed again and then continued. "I remember when I was first fired out the side of a ship, I looked up and there was Nat above the gunwale. Did you know that gunwales are sometimes called saxboards? I should make that the name of a song. So, there I was, about to splinter the side of a ship, and I saw my little brother, Nat, watching out for me. Just like when I went to record with Miles. 'Brother,' he said. 'Go get 'em.' And I did.

"But where is my little brother, now? Where are all those Nats, those other Cannonballs, peppering the sides of ships and crumpled amidst the broken bodies of the enemy?"

The night nurse came in then to change the dressing where my legs once connected to my body. "Nurse, nurse," Cannonball called. "Nurse!"

"Cannonball," she said. "Don't excite yourself. You need to rest."

"But, Nat—where's Nat?" he said. "I need my brother, the corporeal plushness of his cornet, the deep soulful vitality of his songs. I need to know where Nat is?"

Because of Charles's story, I'd forgotten about the chess game.

I looked at the computer screen. Below the board, the cursor blinked, a little white square beating like a heart as he remembered.

Then Charles typed some more.

"In my life, both before and after I lost my legs, I have done many things that I have not been proud of. I have done many good things, yes, certainly, but I did something then that I often think about, especially when I listen to the Cannonball Adderley Quintet, or Miles Davis's classic *Kind of Blue* album, the one where Coltrane and Adderley are the perfect healing ballast to Miles's hurting hipster reticence and introverted only half-aware pain."

A pause and then he typed some more:

"I turned to Cannonball, lying in great discomfort beside me and said, "*I am Nat. Don't you recognize me, brother?*" I said, "Julian, it's me, Nat.""

Bishop to Queen 7. Check.

"And what did Cannonball do then?" I asked Charles. "Did he believe you?"

"I don't know," Charles typed back. "He said nothing. He lay back and died."

King to Bishop 1.

"So," Charles continued. "When the nurse left, I reached over and took his wallet from the night table. I took his money and I took his ID. I became the very same Cannonball who had taken off my legs. But I have been able to live a good life."

"Because of what you did?"

"Because of Cannonball. I bought a wheelchair and I used it. I climbed into it and I rolled through the cities and I rolled through the towns. I rolled right into a lawyers' office in New York City. I got Cannonball's royalties. And I rolled down to the waterside and put the brakes on at the end of a pier. I looked up at the stars and I looked up at the moon. And I knew that because of Cannonball, everything would be all right."

Bishop takes Knight.

Checkmate.

5.

SQUIRREL

When I was a child, my parents replaced me with fog. The fog took my bedroom. My favourite breakfast cereal. The new bike. The fog got grandma's cookies.

Then the fog grew up, began to shave, and got a job. Then it got old. My parents got old, too. When they died, the fog couldn't get up off the sofa but watched TV all day.

After five days, I opened the window and the wind blew the fog away.

I went inside. I chewed up insulation like a squirrel.

THE FALL

She and I are one. We fall asleep in the shower. We fall and our one bum covers the drain. The stall fills with water then falls through the ceiling and lands in the apartment below. We wake in a small pond in an unfamiliar living room. The greetings will soon begin.

THE DOOR

A boy's mother is shot through the front door. The bullet leaves a hole. The hole is a single star in the dark night of the door. The silent throat of the door. The boy puts one of his eyes to the hole and looks out at the world, looks out at the long road leading away. What should we do? the boy asks his father. Buy a new door, the father replies.

PARABLE

Someone broke into a car. The car had a red anti-theft lock wedged across its steering wheel. The thief hot-wired the car and began driving down the road. The police were watching. They followed the car. They turned on their red flashing lights and then their sirens. It was a police chase. It was a high-speed police chase but the thief could only turn the wheel in one direction. Left, he was forced to turn. Then left. Then left again. He could not turn back. Left. His route spiralled in until he had nowhere to go and the police surrounded him. Now's a good time for a parable. Or a lawyer, he thought.

PARLIAMENT

A knock at the door. I open it and there on my steps is Parliament, wrapped against the cold. I lift Parliament, hold it against my chest to make it warm. There, there, you're safe now. No one can harm you. I'll look after you, my little Parliament, my frightened legislative one. I bring Parliament inside and unwrap the blankets. Parliament is scrawny, a lovely chicken, a clock-eyed baby, an institution. My wife warms up a bottle, tests its warmth with an elbow. Parliament is calm now, no bells ringing, nothing but clucks and murmurs. Looking up, its big eyes on me as if I were the world or an election. A Parliament of spit and gurgles, of questions, arguments, love, and feathers.

THE EMPYREAN

During math, a boy puts a pencil up his nose. Another boy whacks the pencil further in, a slim spelunker entering the inaccessible dark of the first boy's head, a small and secret Lascaux at the back of the class. Blurry images of the boy's life. A video game in the long grass, a bus trip along a snowy highway, Twizzlers, and a man waving frantically on the lawn.

The pencil is a yellow joystick. Images are a flurry on the concave whiteboard of the boy's skull, a bony Empyrean limit to the starry dark of the boy's mind.

The second boy begins to write with the pencil, interior cranial graffiti like a whisper in a shouting crowd, an iridescent hork into a midnight sea. It is his name, his joke, his story.

Blood on the knees of the boys and the classroom floor. Hands held to the face. Dark matter. A teacher flailing. An expanding universe of friendship and loss.

PARABLES OF CONVENIENCE

for Beth Bromberg

1.

A man wants to rob a convenience store. He charges in, armed with a knife. He orders the clerk to leave and wait outside. The clerk runs out of the store, calls the police, and never comes back. The police surround the store. They see through the window that the man is eating a chicken.

2.

A man wants to rob his local convenience store. He walks in and chats with the clerk. They both know each other. At a certain point, the man pulls on a black balaclava and holds a gun to the clerk's face. This is a robbery, the man says. I already knew that, the other replies.

3.

A convenience store is unhappy. I could be so much more convenient, it thinks. Late at night it travels to the home of a man who has a balaclava, a gun, and a criminal record. This is a stick-up, the convenience store shouts into the mail slot.

4.

A robber rushes up to the owner of a convenience store just as he's locking up for the night. "Look," he says and shows the owner the handle of a knife that he's put up his sleeve. "One moment, please," the owner says and goes inside to get something. "Look," the owner says, pointing to the toes of a baby sticking out of his own sleeve.

5.

Items on a convenience store shelf want to get stolen. One day, he will come, the toothpaste says.

PLUG

Man walks into a room. A three-prong power socket in an empty wall.

Wow. It hasn't changed at all. I remember it like yesterday. Maybe it *was* yesterday. The things I plugged in. The things I unplugged.

These plugs resemble faces, little surprised faces with open mouths. O, O they say. They seem so innocent.

And I remember a laptop. That time I plugged it in. And a radio and its weather reports. Also, an electrical saw. The things I cut in half. The things I severed.

It's amazing to be back. It's amazing to see it all again. I wonder if…?

He wanders off, then returns with a lamp.

I don't suppose…it couldn't still…

He plugs in the lamp. Nothing. Then he flips the switch on the lamp. It turns on.

Of course. I should have thought of that. Now it really is like old times.

TREE

There was a new boy in our class. The teacher whispered his name but we did not understand. The boy smiled meekly and said nothing. He remained silent during Home Room, Social Studies, and Healthy Snack time. In English class, he shed beautiful almond-shaped leaves. The other children laughed. "Fail," they said.

Recess. He moved to the edge of the playground and stood beside the trees. A kid in the next grade came close and made sawing motions, imitating the growling sounds of a blade on wood, a smirk on his round smooth face. Only the tips of the boy's branches trembled.

After recess was Phys Ed. In the change room, I asked him to repeat his name. "We were not always trees," he said. "Once, my father was a rich man. There were teachers in jeeps and on black horses who rode through the village wielding sharp tongues and axes. They filled water bottles with my father's blood and loaded the jeeps and horses with sacks filled with his money. We were turned into trees. There was nothing left of my father but his dry roots in the hard-packed earth."

We walked down the hall toward the gym. The boy's many branches reached the fluorescent lights and the panelled polystyrene ceiling. There was a delicate scraping as he moved, the footfalls of animals crossing the sky.

"I will avenge my father," he said. "I will return my family to what we were."

On the other side of the steel door, we could hear the boys, panting as they ran across the gym and the voice of the teacher telling them to keep going, to run faster, to think only of running faster. There were a few remaining leaves on the boy's branches. Without meaning to, I leaned in close to the boy and kissed him quickly.

I heard then the sound of a baseball bat breaking across the principal's skull, the books in the library bursting into flame. The boys in the gym became black horses running blindly under the basketball nets, and the teachers turned to ash. The school was an empty field, the boy, a black bird disappearing in a braid of smoke.

I was alone.

HOLIDAY

Grandpa was standing outside the barn, his arms spread, his tongue poking out. The snow fell around him. His loose dressing gown blew behind him like an open road. His eyes were shut. His hair was crows.

We were all there. Billy, Sandy, all the uncles, cousins, aunts, the whole family. A fire blazed in the fireplace, a bustling in and out of the kitchen brought cakes, cookies, coffee to the table. Becky and Matt, my niece and nephew, played a board game on the rug. Will and Ricky ran through the house playing some unintelligible drama. My wife and her sister sat in the kitchen laughing about a family camping trip when they were kids.

We looked all over the house, in the bedrooms, and the basement bathroom, even the garage where he kept his tools, but we couldn't find him.

It was Becky who noticed. "Grandpa's outside!" she said, her hands cupped around her eyes, face pressed to the back window. By this time, only the wet shine of grandpa's head was visible, the tips of his fingers held up towards the dark sky. We ran to the back door, opened it wide. "Grandpa, Grandpa!" Becky shouted. And then he began to move. Arm over arm, Grandpa began to swim first toward the house, then out into the fields, the forgotten cornstalks buried deep in snow, raised arms appearing above the drifts.

"Those who are dead, will still be dead. Those who will die, still will die," Becky said, her breath misting the window.

6.

THE PUNCTUATION OF THIEVES

The semicolon dreams. It isn't one, but two. Brother and sister. Mother and child. Egg and sperm. Zygotic. X and Y. Chromosomal. A Bicameron over the corpus callosum of the page. A greater and lesser brain, brontosaural. A thought and its strange horn. The beginning and end of sleep. A dream of dreaming and of waking. A hand and its other becoming breath and its shadows, a one eye open, a book.

The ampersand dreams. Mother & child, the primordial &, a mother's arms around her child, the Möbius umbilical, the inside out, the turning a portrait of itself, the between one thing and another, the 'and other' connected, the hand and its other, the breath and its shadow, the shadow's curl, the ampersand.

A small island, a curling flame rising, obsidian, a djinn hissing from the prison of its tittle.

An exclamation mark bent by the wind, a cupped hand seeking purchase on the sleek face of the page.

A streamer or the path of the kite and its flyer, the full stop and its single ear, the question mark is an attempt to pull something in, to connect by asking, the angler of grammar, certainty growing an antler at sentence end.

The question mark is an ouroboros snake the moment before catching its own tail. An inverted nose, a one-eyed bass clef, a quest which turns back, questioning as a dog circles twice before sleep.

The pirate dances: a jazz hook oscillates, marking an interrogative spot in the thought map of thin air.

Small star. Asshole. Firework burst. Cobweb scaffold, the spider gone. Footnote from a distant constellation that may exist no longer. Doleful snowflake: matchless star in a storm of a single flurry.

We take different paths from a single place yet return from diverse journeys to the same centre. Or we wander the compass: our paths cross and we move on. The horizon surrounds us, our single scrunched and winking eye.

Six-pointed: first position three-toed ballet. W and its pond other. A bedful of Xs, their bodies entangled. Five-pointed: endless knot, pentacle, little headless man, leaf spine.

A tiger in dreams. A railway car. Things and their inner shape. Matter and the beams of its being, a mark of more than one way of seeing the spot.

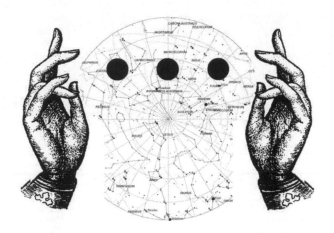

Ellipsis juggling, the most difficult trick in the repertoire. A juggling of what's not there, what's lost, left out, erased, or forgotten. And the juggler must keep each of the three elements perfectly in line with a ground that she cannot see, like black holes precisely aligned in empty space and yet parallel with the curved horizon of a distant earth.

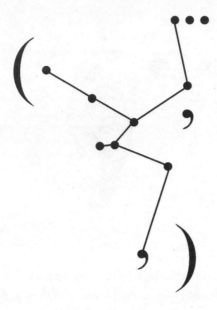

DARK MATTER PUNCTUATION

1.

A hidden comma curled like a seahorse in the mind. Wraithlike periods, ghostly ellipses, the semi-colons, albino and invisible, spectres of phantom punctuation, the incorporeal spirits of the mouth, gathering the breathless-ness of thought, run-on and undivided, as if between the narrow hands of parentheses.

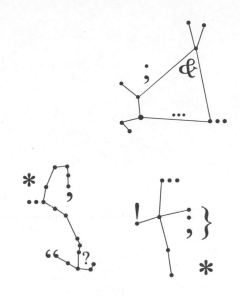

2.

If the written word is weather fallen from the troposphere of speech, punctuation, rising from the apostrosphere, is the seasons, giving shape to the spoken year with its ecliptic and paradoxes, its long summer dashes, its bitter winter of exclamations. Grammar, the pre-emptive counsel of language before the chaos of the mouth.

3.

What would a sesqui-colon look like? A deca-colon? A giga-colon?

The dark matter of punctuation, the metaphysic breath, the beginning, the ending, the between of things. An almost infinite antimatter of punctuation, a predomination of quotation marks, "air quotes where there is no air," language speaking the world into being with care, compassion, inadvertence, pity, irony.

!

The single horn of the exclamation mark, the shadow of a unicorn surmounted by its long eburnean shadow, a distant comet and its swart trail. A flashing darkness riding through the bright forest.

A finger raised to test the wind, a short then long dash, morse code aspiring upwards, exclaiming toward the sky.

Is it an instruction: "exclaim here," or a regret?: "it would have been a good thing to fill the preceding word with unbridled joy, or shouting."

The mark itself an exclamation, the midge of the full stop stretched out, a throat, a smear, a cone of explosion.

A skid and then a sudden stop, long life/short end or vice versa, a sundial gnomon and its shadow tongue painted by light.

Death's favourite punctuation: the jot, a single moment, its long black robe fluttering behind, the letter of self, inverted.

●

At the end of a sentence a period, a full stop. Peer into its darkness, a celestial sky so dark nothing is visible save the darkness itself.

Or it's some kind of cave, an inscrutable Lascaux, a dim basement. Jazz musicians crowd beside bison hunters. Hear the shimmer of the cymbal and the erotic bleat of the saxophone, the clink of mouth-bound martini glasses, the soft murmur of warriors.

Now lean closer, look as if through the aperture of a microscope. There's an entire city. A single swart cell. An inkwell. The birthmark of the sentence. An insect whose legs my brother removed. You raise your head and look out at the room. Black ink from a silent movie gag circles your eye.

7.

SMALL TEETH

Last night I slept with the Tooth Fairy, woke up with tinsel on my back, dreamed that my jaw was broken and I could remember the touch of her lacy wings on my chest. She put her tiara on my night table, her wand under the bed.

Where was my wife? She was flying alone in the cloudless sky, carrying a grocery cart filled with the newly plucked feathers of trumpeter swans. She had left me a note, saying "When the Tooth Fairy comes, I've left out cookies and Scotch. You may take her to our bed. I'm off to see Abe Lincoln, when he was a young lawyer, and without the beard."

"Was the Tooth Fairy good in bed?" my friends ask.

"Not bad. Better than Peter Pan or Mrs. Santa," I say. "And she can fly, you know."

Really, she was great, and all my teeth fell out and she replaced them, one by one, with the bones of small birds. I open and close my mouth: a robin creasing the sky above my yard, a sparrow's quick wings.

It was like the time I snuck into Walmart dressed in the skin of a dog. I was looking for garden ornaments. For accessories for my car. For something to stop me waking the neighbours at four a.m. with my howling.

"You're not really a dog," the Tooth Fairy says. She is in the plumbing aisle, looking for nails.

"Yes, I know," I reply. "I'm a wolf and it seems I've left my money in my other skin."

The Tooth Fairy looks at me, tears forming in her white eyes. "When you were losing teeth, you seemed like such a good boy. Always left a nice, well-written note under your pillow. Always spent the money I gave you wisely. And to think, here you are, dressed in the skin of a dog, barking at bird feeders, at rubberized car mats, sinking your teeth into tires and contemplating ostentatious hubcaps emblazoned with lions' teeth.

"Save your money," she says. "It is the beginning of the twenty-first century and you will need every cent, even the ones with Abe Lincoln on the back."

She touches my head with her wand. I open my mouth and pennies fall out from where they have collected on my tongue. My arms have become like wings, their feathers the feathery pages of the telephone book, opened to page 247: Dr. Greenblatt, Orthodontist, 251-1457.

I am the Sphinx, a griffin, Osiris. In the before-dawn darkness of my skull, small points of light illuminate my brain. A hawk flies silently from one ear to the other. The twin moons of my eyes are eclipsed by dark lids. The silver net of a shopping cart glints as it crosses between the lobes of my brain. My wife has been shopping and she has filled her cart with small teeth.

THE TELL-TALE HEART RETOLD: A TALE TOLD BY HEART

We live in a rented room on the ground floor of our landlord's house. The old man sleeps. Wakes. Stays in bed gathering warmth like a pile of old leaves. Sometimes he moves to the chair by the fire. The landlord brings him tea in the late afternoon. The newspaper. A book. We are in the closing chapters when the adventure is over. We are the four red chambers of the old man's heart, a drum down a dark well. A drum tolling over distant hills.

But we did not know the landlord was insane. Not until it was too late. But a heart lives in darkness. Our world is a cave. Outside we hear murmurs, voices. His voice. The muffled bell of a tram. An axe striking wood, a thump like a heartbeat. And inside, the old man's ribs are a cage, an alternation of light and dark, dark and light, like the lines of shadow and sun deep in a forest of leafless trees.

We beat steadily. We do not stop. It is a persistent march into night, then day, then night again. The trudging alternation of dark and light. We keep on. We do not relent. A heart beats because we know what we must do. A heart beats so we move forward. A heart beats. We know what we must do. A heart beats and now that we are old, we feel it more intensely. We hear each beat and remember. When we were young, we did not count each dance step, each footfall, each pump of the heart, the warm blood creeping around inside the flesh. Now each beat is measured and deliberate, deep like a tomb door closing. And so we keep on before it closes forever.

We did not know the landlord was insane. At least, not until it was too late.

For seven nights, each night after the chiming of midnight, he creeps toward our room. The latch lifted, he opens the door a head's width only. We hear him muttering. His weaselly breathing, his obsequious mewling. There is a faint flickering of lantern-light as he listens to the old man's sighs. A heart beats. He believes that we are asleep. But inside, we are beating. The slow clock ticking, the hours of a life.

We did not know the landlord was insane. Seven long nights, he creeps into our room to watch and listen to the old man. And the old man's eye. It is nothing but the eye of an old man but, still, it frightens the landlord as he watches, though it remains closed as the old man sleeps. The old man's old eye, staring out as the landlord greets us pleasantly in the morning, asks the old man how he slept. How he slept indeed. The old man's eye is vulture blue, the colour one might imagine a mystic third eye. But age needs no such sorcerous folderol. It is its own third eye, understanding time and the slow supernatural unfolding of the body. The third eye of age which knows the beating of the subterranean heart. The heart in the body beating like a hammer on an anvil. A heart beats and we temper the days with such beating.

The landlord returns each midnight for seven nights. We did not know he was insane. His breathing faster, anxious, irregular. An animal trapped by its own fear. The old man sleeps and yet we march on, a sentry pacing the parapet of blood and ribs. Then the landlord's finger slips and the lantern knocks against the door frame. The old man starts. Sits up. "Who is it?" he calls. "Who is there?" But the landlord remains silent with the lantern closed. The old man strains to see in the darkness. "Who is there?" he says again. Heartbeat. Heartbeat. We are as a bass drum in this parade of fear and dread. Heartbeat. The old man does not lie back but remains staring, his eyes blind, but open.

Hours pass. One o'clock. We mark them with our dull but quickening tolling. Two o'clock. The door moves slowly, opening almost imperceptibly.

Three o'clock. The landlord enters our room. Heartbeat. The light from his lantern a single beam and all is dark but the old man's eye. Heartbeat. The eye does not move but fixes on the man in the doorway. The old man's eye fixes the man in the doorway with the unforgiving gaze of a hawk. The breath is held. Nothing moves. Heartbeat. Time itself is marked only by the crescendo of our beating. It is as if this beating would burst the old man's chest and fill the room with his beating. His chest the dark room around us, and our pumping shaking its walls. A red knot of muscle unfurling, pressing the landlord and his lantern against the door. Our beating the raging of a giant's fist. Our beating, as if the endless bell of heaven were sounding. As if time itself and Death's infinite axe were ringing.

The landlord leaps into the room with a banshee wail. He is upon us. And in a moment, the heavy bed is overturned, the old man trapped beneath. A gasp. A sigh. A last breath. The old man asleep forever.

But we keep beating because a heart must keep beating. A heart knows what it must do. The landlord takes the old man—the dead weight of his body—from under the bed and drags him across the floor. With his axe, he cuts the body to pieces, like a tree turned to firewood. He lifts three floorboards and drops the severed body into darkness. Replaces the boards. We keep beating. A heart inside the torso of a corpse inside a narrow cave beneath the floor. There are sounds above us. The bed moving. We know what we must do. Men's voices. Police. "There is nothing here," the landlord says. "We are alone," he says. The policemen mutter. We keep beating. Beneath the floor. His heart, beating. "Nothing here," the landlord says. His heart, beating. Beneath the floor, beating. Beneath the floor, we know what we must do. "There is nothing," the landlord shouts. His heart, beating. Beneath the floor, we keep beating. "It is clean here," the landlord wails. "There is nothing." We keep beating. We know what we must do. His heart, beating. We know what we must do. Beneath the floor, the landlord wails. We know what we must do.

We keep beating. We know what we must do. Beneath the floor, we know what we must do. His heart, beating, the landlord wails. We know what we must do.

ALBERT'S PARADISE

Now the sun rose higher and the heat of the day increased. The whole company remained in the pleasant shade, and, as a thousand birds sang among the verdant branches, someone asked Francesco to play the organ a little, to see whether the sound would make the birds increase or diminish their song. He did so at once, and a great wonder followed—for when the sound of the organ began, many of the birds were seen to fall silent and gather around as if in amazement, listening for a long time; and then they resumed their song and redoubled it, showing inconceivable delight, especially one nightingale, who came and perched above the organ, on a branch over Francesco's head.

Hey, Frank, it said, that's pretty good, for a human. Why don't you have another cup of coffee? I know it's pretty hot out here, but when you pour the milk I'll have an opportunity to tell you about Bessie, the cow whose milk it is. Why, I've seen her conducting, I think it was the Vienna Philharmonic. I know what you're thinking: you don't often see a female conducting an orchestra. But Bessie's different. No one does Mahler like she does, though it's true they have to stop when her udders get full and she needs to be milked.

And Frank, a word about these other birds here, redoubling their song in inconceivable delight. Well, don't be fooled. You should see how they act when Stevie Wonder is around.

Did I ever show you how I can eat a worm and sing at the same time? Hey, maybe later you'll come on over to the verdant glade, just past the river, and play Twister with the beasts of the field and the other birds of the air. You should see how the garter snakes make a lattice of themselves, while the sparrows, each of them like a summer flower, bedeck it. It's really not bad, what with the deer singing their sweet little R&B songs and the blind moles coming up from their underground tunnels, dressed in flashy clothes, telling tales of Milan and Ferrara in the sixteenth century.

Anyway, I've come to ask about Albert. I haven't seen him in a while, not since we went south.

It's like this, Frank. Once, me and a bunch of other birds, a flock really, made ourselves little harnesses hewn of spiderweb and then attached Albert to us with blades of grass. The sun was a giant yolk in the centre of the sky's blue egg, and we pulled up into the wind. There we were, speeding over fields, cutting off blue jays, careening around clouds. Albert hung beneath us in his grass nest like a gunner in an old warplane. He was singing and calling out to the surprised farmers in the fields below, "I am the sky's tractor, a dolphin of the air. I am Pegasus, my wings of nightingale made. Nothing, not even shag carpeting, can soar as I soar."

And we birds, we knew how he felt. Once, we rode a city bus downtown, and once, some of us travelled the Sea of Galilee in a glass-bottomed boat. A bunch of us have even been in the trunk of a Lamborghini as it sped down the Autobahn. When the driver, a certain Mr. Beerbaum, opened the trunk to get his suitcase, we burst out, each of us carrying an apple in our claws, apples that Mr. Beerbaum was bringing home to his mother, who made the kind of succulent apple pie that any bird would delight in flying out of, as if from the trunk of an expensive Italian car.

All night we sailed across the sky with Albert beneath us. We were a web of birds, and Albert, tied by the sticky threads of grass, was our catch. As the moon rose, the shadows of nightingales flickered across his sleeping face. He was dreaming he was a lawn chair sitting by the pool. Through the living room's open window, he could hear his wife playing "Midnight in Moscow" on the organ and he hummed along.

By the time we passed over Algeria, Albert had woken up. We flew far above the clouds, hardly moving our wings so that Albert could shave. "Where are you taking me?" he asked. "I feel like a walnut cabinet, or chewing gum on a basketball player's chair."

We birds were in a convivial mood and so we joked with him. "Knock knock," we said. "There was an Irishman, an Italian, and a Jew. What do you get if you lift a Canadian in the grassy arms of nightingales flying south across the desert?"

I want you to know, Frank, though it's hard to understand, sitting here playing organ in the pleasant shade, Albert taught us a lot. He taught us the words to "The Star-Spangled Banner," told us about Tintern Abbey and Saskatchewan. He explained about salt.

You should know that the time we spent carrying Albert across the earth was a time of song, of quiet speech, of croissants and coffee. We learned how to use a wheelbarrow, a compass, how to make food crisp in a FryDaddy.

And we, in our turn, taught Albert. We showed him the vulture's ten-speed, the tears of the sobbing moon. We explained how to make a dining room table from camel skin, how the jackals like teak veneer. We taught him to recognize Iceland by its shadow, how to cut down trees by sound.

In the time Albert spent below us, he learned what the web-bound chests of nightingales know, exhausted and flying for weeks on only coffee, the occasional croissant.

And yes, have another coffee, Frank. You deserve it. Let me tell you that though Bessie's Mahler was good, her Wagner was terrific. The tilt of her head, a movement of her broad nose, and they wept for hours in the balconies' dim light.

In fact, it was Bessie's idea for us to take Albert over the earth in his cradle. She phoned from a tour of New Mexico. "Take Albert beneath you," she said, "over the ocean's bevelled floor. Take him," she said, "over Europe and across Africa's blond plain."

Though presidents and prime ministers have invited us skiing, and we're consulted by butchers and priests, it was to Bessie we listened that rain-dappled day. A letter was sent to Albert to which he replied, "I will dress as a heavy-weight boxer. Frank will play the organ while I'm away. Your voices are like the song 'Midnight in Moscow,' performed by mimes. I am not, nor have I ever been. Thank you. Thank you. Thank you."

ORIGINAL SKIN

Night. Nine-thirty.

Looks like sperm, the Rabbi thought, entranced by the rain hitting the window and dribbling down at high speed. Most drops were quickly swept away by the wipers, but every so often, one made it down to the hood.

And he remembered a T-shirt worn by some guy jogging past his house. On the shirt, one sperm had broken away, the clear leader of a pack of sperm, approaching a large egg near the neckline. "Only the strong survive," the caption read.

"Look," his wife Tanya said, nodding at a sign. "A hundred miles to Nashville."

"That's good," he said. "I'm tired. A little supper and then let's get right to bed."

An hour earlier, Tanya had taken over driving. He hadn't slept well the night before and had got up early. This was a rare trip without their—what seemed like—five hundred children. Another child was growing inside his wife. One of the ones that survived, peace be upon them. It'd be three more months before the child would swim—or be pushed—toward the light. He'd let Tanya sleep late this morning while he took care of the kids and prepared things for his mother-in-law to stay over for the weekend.

It had been raining for days.

Ten o'clock.

As they drove, his wife began to recount her strange morning dream:

A man chasing her on a long train. He was disguised as the rabbi, her husband, and he knew the seven secret words for sex. For everything. This rabbi/

not-rabbi had been sharing a lemon meringue pie with his old friend, the Catholic schoolteacher. With a shout, he ripped off his disguise and began to kiss her, getting meringue all over. Then she escaped. The other passengers were Nazis with human faces and they all had library cards. Jewish library cards. The train had been born from between her legs. Inside the club car, her five hundred children threw food at each other and now an SS officer was trying to kiss her while she played the banjo. The man disguised as her husband smashed through the little window of the club car door. She was terrified. His face, his voice, his body had become identical to her husband's. He began to sing prayers but he sounded far away.

"So, Rabbi, tell me," she asked her husband. "What do you think it means?"

"We should make love tonight?" he asked.

Ten-thirty.

The road was dark and the rain continued to spatter against the windshield. The oncoming cars and trucks came out of nowhere, shooting up water, and frightening her with their speed as they flashed past.

"I packed some sandwiches," she said.

"Corned beef," I hope.

"Why don't you look?" she said. He leaned forward and opened up the bag.

"Ah. Corned beef."

"Yeah, and some of the kugel Franny brought over the other night."

"A dream dinner."

Eleven o'clock.

They drove in silence. They didn't see the minivan swerve into their lane until it was right in front of them.

He woke to find the two vans fused together in a mess of contorted metal.

"Tanya," the Rabbi said, but she and the baby were lost, crushed between the crumpled vans.

The rabbi tried to move. His legs didn't work. He could see a small child through the fractured glass of the other van. A vague pink opalescence. A little girl, a toddler, probably two years old. And she was dying.

He reached through the window and pulled the girl close to him.

With the knife meant for the kugel, he cut his chest open and pushed her inside. His broken body would become her second skin and a two-year-old girl would become the father of what seemed like five hundred, soon to seem like five hundred-and-one, and the husband of his beautiful dead wife and child. He would watch from somewhere, from nowhere, from outside, as she woke in his paraplegic body, as the people in the emergency vehicles pulled up on the road beside the trees and began working to save anyone they could. And then, like the rain, he'd be gone.

NOTES

The numerical sequence '251-1457' dates back to that Arcadian pre-cellular time when seven digit phone numbers roamed the earth and area-codeless communication with orthodontists was possible.

Quotation in "Albert's Paradise" from Giovanni da Prato, *Paradiso degli Alberti* (ca. 1425) cited in Donald J. Grout and Claude Palisca, *A History of Western Music*, 4th ed. (New York: W.W. Norton, 1988), 155.

"Polar Bear" is for Robert Dziekański

ACKNOWLEDGEMENTS

I, Dr. Greenblatt would like to thank Stuart Ross for his invaluable textual flossing of many of these texts as well as for his more prosaic insights; Conan Tobias who enthusiastically birthed several of these pieces in his *Taddle Creek Magazine*; David Lee with whom many of these stories have been made live with his toothsome music; Brian Kaufman for his keen editorial overbite and skillful polishing; Karen Green and Shazia Hafiz Ramji for diverse feats Anvilar; my wife, Beth Bromberg for things too numerous to recount; my children, Aaron, Ryan, and Rudi, for their complex enthusiasms and insights; and Dr. Ivan Wambera for moving my teeth when I was a child.

"The Hand" (with Jenna Mariash) and "The Sleep of Elephants" have been made into short films available on the "Gary Barwin" channel on YouTube.

Some of these texts previously appeared in:

Drunken Boat, Papirmass, Taddle Creek Magazine, The Olive Reading Series editions, The Barnstormer, The Rusty Toque, subTerrain, A Title Knows No Tales (Grey Borders), *Dragnet, Prose of the Day* (Upstart, Ireland), *The Incongruous Quarterly, Wonk, This Magazine, Joyland, Twaddle Magazine, Crash, Undercurrents Journal, The Goose, Arc Poetry Magazine, Canadian Poetry Magazine,*

LemonHound, and in *The Boneshaker Anthology, Dragnet Anthology, the Puritan Compendium, Scream Instant Anthology, Rogue Stimulus*, and *From Sinai to the Shtetl and Beyond.* "Small Teeth" previously appeared in *Big Red Baby* (The Mercury Press, 1998) and "The Saxophonists Book of the Dead" was released as a serif of nottingham chapbook.

I'd like to thank all those involved with these publications as well as those organizing the many reading series in which many of these texts were performed. I'm grateful to be part of a vigorous and inspiring literary community. I'd also like to thank those supporters of public funding for the arts for helping to provide assistance to me and my publishers through the Ontario Arts Council, the Canada Council, the British Columbia Arts Council as well through other governmental programs.

GARY BARWIN is a writer, composer, multimedia artist, and educator and the author of eighteen books of poetry and fiction as well as books for both teens and children. His work has been widely performed, broadcast, anthologized and published nationally and internationally.

Recent books include *Moon Baboon Canoe* (poetry, Mansfield Press, 2014) and *The Wild and Unfathomable Always* (vispo, Xexoxial Editions, 2015). Other books include *Franzlations* (with Hugh Thomas and Craig Conley; New Star), *The Obvious Flap* (with Gregory Betts; BookThug) and *The Porcupinity of the Stars* (Coach House.) A novel, *Yiddish for Pirates* is forthcoming from Random House Canada (2016). He is the editor of *Sonosyntactics: The New and Selected Poems of Paul Dutton* (Laurier Poetry Series) which will appear in Fall 2015. He was Young Voices eWriter-in-Residence at the Toronto Public Library in Fall of 2013 and Writer-in-Residence at Western University in 2014-2015. Barwin received a PhD (music composition) from SUNY at Buffalo.

Barwin was the recipient of the 2013 City of Hamilton Arts Award (Writing), the Hamilton Poetry Book of the Year 2001 and 2011 and co-winner of 2011 Harbourfront Poetry NOW competition, the 2010 bpNichol chapbook award, the KM Hunter Artist Award, and the President's Prize for Poetry (York University). His young adult fiction has been shortlisted for both the Canadian Library Association YA Book of the Year and the Arthur Ellis Award. He has received major grants from the Canada Council and the Ontario Arts Council for his work.

He lives in Hamilton, Ontario and at garybarwin.com.